SECRETS OF A CAREER GIRL

BY
CAROL MARINELLI

Published in Great Britain 2013
by Mills & Boon, an imprint of Harlequin (UK) Limited.
Large Print edition 2014
Harlequin (UK) Limited, Eton House,
18-24 Paradise Road, Richmond, Surrey, TW9 1SR

© 2013 Carol Marinelli

ISBN: 978 0 263 23849 5

Harlequin (UK) Limited's policy is to use papers that
are natural, renewable and recyclable products and made
from wood grown in sustainable forests. The logging
and manufacturing processes conform to the legal
environmental regulations of the country of origin.

Printed and bound in Great Britain
by CPI Antony Rowe, Chippenham, Wiltshire

He pulled up on his elbow and gave her a kiss. It was a bit pointless to pretend it was a friendly one, given they were lying on the bed, but Ethan did kiss her with no intention other than to say goodbye.

Except he'd forgotten how much he liked kissing her till he was back there, and Penny was remembering all over again, and his mouth was so nice and his hands started to wander—and then he checked himself.

'Sorry.'

'For what?'

'Taking things too far.'

'You've never taken things too far,' Penny said. 'You haven't taken things far enough.'

'Penny…' He took her face in his hands and wrestled with indecision, not sure if it was Hot Mess Penny he was talking to, whom he completely adored and could deal with, or Baby-Making Mode Penny, who terrified him so.

She got it.

'I'm not asking you to get me pregnant…'

'I know.'

Dear Reader

I really enjoyed writing Penny and Jasmine's stories which make up my SECRETS ON THE EMERGENCY WING duet. Even though they are sisters they are very different and that is what made them so real to me. I loved that, even though they had the same parents and shared the same pasts, because of their unique personalities they looked at things differently.

Penny and Jasmine don't look alike; they don't even get on. No one could even guess that they are sisters— they really are two different sides of the same coin. Yet, for all their differences, there are similarities and I had a lot of fun with a little secret of Penny's that you shan't find out till near the end of the second book.

I really would love to know which sister ends up being your favourite? Except, as my mother tells me, you're not allowed to have favourites…

You may yet be surprised ☺

Happy reading!

Carol

x

SECRETS ON THE EMERGENCY WING

Life and love—
behind the doors of an Australian ER

Book 1 in Carol Marinelli's
SECRETS ON THE EMERGENCY WING duet

DR DARK AND FAR-TOO DELICIOUS

is also available this month

The **SECRETS ON THE EMERGENCY WING**
duet is also available in eBook format
from www.millsandboon.co.uk

Carol Marinelli recently filled in a form where she was asked for her job title and was thrilled, after all these years, to be able to put down her answer as 'writer'. Then it asked what Carol did for relaxation and, after chewing her pen for a moment, Carol put down the truth—'writing'. The third question asked, 'What are your hobbies?' Well, not wanting to look obsessed or, worse still, boring, she crossed the fingers on her free hand and answered 'swimming and tennis'. But, given that the chlorine in the pool does terrible things to her highlights, and the closest she's got to a tennis racket in the last couple of years is watching the Australian Open, I'm sure you can guess the real answer!

Recent books by Carol Marinelli:

Mills & Boon® Medical Romance™

NYC ANGELS: REDEEMING THE PLAYBOY**
SYDNEY HARBOUR HOSPITAL:
  AVA'S RE-AWAKENING*
HERS FOR ONE NIGHT ONLY?
CORT MASON—DR DELECTABLE
HER LITTLE SECRET
ST PIRAN'S: RESCUING PREGNANT CINDERELLA†
KNIGHT ON THE CHILDREN'S WARD

**NYC Angels
**Sydney Harbour Hospital*
†*St Piran's Hospital*

Mills & Boon® Modern™ Romance

PLAYING THE DUTIFUL WIFE
BEHOLDEN TO THE THRONE~
BANISHED TO THE HAREM~
AN INDECENT PROPOSITION
A SHAMEFUL CONSEQUENCE
HEART OF THE DESERT
THE DEVIL WEARS KOLOVSKY

~*Empire of the Sands*

**These books are also available in eBook format
from www.millsandboon.co.uk**

PROLOGUE

THE PATIENTS LIKED her, though.

Emergency Consultant Ethan Lewis glanced up as an elderly lady in a wheelchair, with a younger woman pushing her, approached the nurses' station and asked if Penny Masters was working today. The lady in the wheelchair still had her wristband on and was holding a bag of discharge medications and a tin of chocolates.

'I think she's on her lunch break,' answered Lisa, the nurse unit manager. 'I'll just buzz around and find out.'

'No, don't disturb her. Mum just wanted to give her these to say thank you—she really was marvellous that day when Mum was brought in.'

'It's no problem,' Lisa said, picking up a phone. 'I think she's in her office.'

Yes, Ethan thought to himself. Unlike everybody else, who took their lunch in the staffroom, Penny would be holed away in her office, catching up with work. He'd been trying to have a word with her all day—a casual word, to ask a favour—but, as Ethan was starting to discover, there was no such thing as a casual word with Penny.

Ethan had been working in the emergency department of the Peninsula Hospital for more than three months now. It was a busy bayside hospital that serviced some of Melbourne's outer suburbs. The emergency department was, for the most part, a friendly one, which suited Ethan's laid-back ways.

For the most part.

He watched as Penny walked over. Immaculate as ever, petite and slender, her very straight blonde hair was tied back neatly and she was wearing a three-quarter-sleeve navy wraparound dress and smart low-heeled shoes. The female equivalent of a business suit perhaps, which was rather unusual in this place—most of the other staff, Ethan included, preferred the comfort and ease of wearing scrubs. Penny, though, dressed smartly at all times and gloved and gowned up for everything.

'Mrs Adams, how lovely to see you looking so well.' Ethan watched as she approached her ex-patient. Without being told, Penny knew her name. Though the greeting was friendly, it was a very professional smile that Penny gave and there was no tactile embrace. Penny stood there and enquired how Mrs Adams was doing with more than mere polite interest, because even though they had clearly just left the ward, the daughter had a few questions about her mother's medication and Penny went through the medication bag and easily answered all of them.

'Thank you so much for explaining,' Mrs Adams's daughter said. 'I didn't like to keep asking the nurse when I didn't understand.'

'You *must* keep asking.'

Yes, the patients loved Penny.

They didn't mind in the least that she was meticulous, thorough and incredibly inflexible in her treatment plans.

It was the staff that struggled—if Penny wanted observations every fifteen minutes, she accepted no excuses if they weren't done. If Penny ordered analgesia, it didn't matter to her that there might be a line-up at the drug trolley, or that there was no one available to check the dose, because her patient needed it now.

Penny walked Mrs Adams and her daughter to the exit, and stood talking for another couple of moments there. As she walked back through the department, Jasmine, a nurse who also happened to be Penny's sister, called her over to the nurses' station.

'What did you get?' Jasmine asked.

Penny glanced down at the tin she was holding. 'Chocolate macadamias,' she said, peeling off the Cellophane. 'I'll leave them here for everyone to help themselves.'

She wasn't even that friendly towards her sister, Ethan thought as Penny put down the chocolates on the bench and went to go. He would never have picked Penny and Jasmine as sisters—it had had to be pointed out to him.

Jasmine was dark and curvy, Penny blonde and very slim.

Jasmine smiled and was friendly, whereas Penny was much more guarded and standoffish. Ethan refused to play by her silent, stay-back rules and he called her as she went to head off. 'Can I have a quick word, Penny?'

'I'm actually at lunch,' Penny said.

The very slow burning Taurus within Ethan stirred a little then—his hazel eyes flashed and, had there been horns hidden under his thick black hair, Penny would now be seeing her first glimpse of them. It took a lot to rile Ethan, but Penny was starting to. Ethan had always known that there might be a problem when he had taken this job—two of the department's senior registrars had also applied for the consultant position.

Jasmine's new husband Jed was one of them.

Penny the other.

Knowing the stiff competition, Ethan had been somewhat taken aback when he had been offered the role. He had since learnt that Jed had taken a job in a city hospital, but Penny was still here and, yes, it was awkward. Ethan often reminded himself that her ego might be a touch fragile and that it might take a little while for her to accept him in the role that she had applied for.

Well, it was time that Penny did accept who was boss and, for the first time, Ethan pulled rank as she went to head back to her lunch.

'That's fine.' He looked into her cool blue eyes. 'But when you're finished, can you make sure that you come and find me? I need to speak with you.'

She hesitated for just a second before answering. 'Regarding what?'

No, there was no such thing as a casual word with Penny. 'I'm on call next weekend,' Ethan said. 'Is there any chance that you could cover me for a few hours on Sunday afternoon? I'm hop-

ing to go to a football match with my cousin—'
He was about to explain further, but before he
could, Penny interrupted him.

'I've already got plans.'

She didn't add 'sorry'.

Penny never did.

As she turned to go Ethan's jaw clamped down
and, rarely for him, his temper was rising. He
was tempted to tap her on the shoulder and tell
her that this was more than some idle request
because his team was playing that weekend. His
cousin was actually on the waiting list for a heart
transplant.

No, he wouldn't waste the sympathy card
on her and with good reason—Ethan actually
smiled a twisted smile as Penny walked off.

'Did you use it?' Phil would ask when Ethan
rang him tonight.

'*Nope.*'

'Good,' Phil would say. 'Save it for women
you fancy.'

Yes, it was a black game, but one that got Phil through and gave them both a few laughs.

He certainly wouldn't be using the sympathy card on Penny.

'We're going to the airport to see Mum off on Sunday.' Jasmine had jumped down from her stool to help herself to the chocolate nuts and offered an explanation where her sister had offered none. She was trying to smooth things over, Ethan guessed, for her socially awkward sister. Except Penny wasn't awkward, Ethan decided—she simply wasn't the least bit sociable. 'It's been planned for ages.'

'It's not a problem.' Ethan got back to his notes as Jasmine, taking another handful of the chocolate nuts, headed off, but as he reached to take a handful himself Ethan realised that Penny hadn't even taken one.

She could use the sugar, Ethan thought darkly.

'You could try asking Gordon,' Lisa suggested when it was just the two of them, because Ethan had told her while chatting a few days ago about his cousin, and, no, he hadn't been using the sympathy card with Lisa!

'I'll see,' Ethan said. Gordon had three sons and another baby on the way. 'Though he probably needs his weekend with his family, as does Penny.' He couldn't keep the tart edge from his voice as he mentioned her name.

'You don't know, do you?' Lisa was trying to sort out the nursing roster but she too had seen the frosty exchange between Penny and Ethan, and though she could see both sides, Lisa understood both sides too. 'Jasmine and Penny's mum was brought in a few months ago in full cardiac arrest. They were both on duty at the time.'

Ethan grimaced. To anyone who worked in Emergency, dealing with someone you knew, especially a family member, was the worst-case scenario. 'Did you manage to keep it from them?'

'Hardly! Well, we kept it from Jasmine while the resuscitation was happening so at least she found out rather more kindly than Penny did.'

Lisa put down her pen and told Ethan what had happened that day.

'Penny was just pulling on her gown when the paramedics wheeled her mother in,' Lisa said. 'You know how she gowns up all the time.' Lisa rolled her eyes. 'Penny takes up half of the laundry budget on gowns alone. Anyway, you know how she usually starts snapping out orders and things? Well, I knew that there was something wrong because she just stood there frozen. She asked for Jed—he was the other registrar on that day—but he was stuck with another patient. Penny told me that the patient was her mum and then just snapped out of it and got on with the resuscitation, just as if it were any other patient. And she kept going until we got Mr Dean here to take over. She did tell me not to let Jasmine in, though.'

Lisa gave a wry smile. 'I didn't even know, till that point, that Penny and Jasmine were sisters. Penny likes to keep her personal life well away from work.'

'I had noticed.'

'The cruise is a huge thing for their mother. Do you see now why Penny couldn't swap?'

'I do,' Ethan said, and got back to his notes. But that was the problem exactly—he'd never have heard it from Penny herself.

And then he stopped writing, took another handful of chocolate nuts as it dawned on him...

Like him, Penny had refused to play the sympathy card.

CHAPTER ONE

'HAVE YOU THOUGHT about letting a few people at work know what's going on?'

Penny closed her eyes at her sister's suggestion and didn't respond. The very last thing Penny wanted was the people at work to know that she was going through IVF.

Again.

It was bad enough for the intensely private Penny that her mum and sister knew but, given that Penny was seriously petrified of needles, she'd had no choice but to confide in Jasmine, who would be giving Penny her evening injections soon.

While she couldn't get through it without Jasmine's practical help, there were times when

Penny wished that she had never let on that she was trying for a baby.

Yes, her family had been wonderfully supportive but sometimes Penny didn't want to talk about it. She didn't want to hear that they were keeping their fingers crossed for her, didn't always want to give the required permanent updates and, more than anything, she had hated the sympathy when it hadn't worked out the first time. Naturally they had tried to comfort her and understand what they could not—they had both had babies.

The two sisters were walking along the beach close to where they both lived. Penny lived in one of the smart townhouses that had gone up a couple of years ago and took in the glittering bay views. Jasmine lived a little further along the beach with her new husband Jed and her toddler son Simon, who was from Jasmine's first marriage. The newlyweds were busily house hunting and trying to find somewhere suitable between the city, where Jed now worked, and the Peninsula Hospital.

Now, though, the sisters lived close by and, having waved their mother off from Melbourne airport for her long-awaited overseas trip, they walked along the beach with Simon, enjoying the last hour of sunlight.

'It might be a good idea to let a couple of people in on what you're going through,' Jasmine pushed, because she wanted Penny to have the support Jasmine felt that she needed, especially as Penny was going through this all alone.

'Even my own friends don't really understand,' Penny said. 'Coral thinks I'm being selfish, and Bianca, though she says I should go for it if that's what I want…' Her voice trailed off. 'If I can't talk about it with my own friends, what's it going to be like at work?'

'Lisa especially would be really good.'

'Lisa is a nurse unit manager,' Penny broke in. 'I'm not a nurse.'

'She runs the place, though,' Jasmine said. 'She'd be able to look out for you a little bit.'

'I don't need looking out for.'

Jasmine wasn't so sure. She could see that the treatment was taking its toll on her sister, not that Penny would appreciate her observations.

Jasmine wanted so badly to help her sister. They had never really been close but Penny had always looked out for her—several years older, Penny had shielded her from the worst of their parents' rows and their mother's upset when their father had finally left. It had been the same when their mother had been brought into Emergency—Penny had made sure Jasmine hadn't found out about their mother in the same way that she had.

'I know this is all a bit new to you, Jasmine,' Penny said. 'But I've been living with this for years. I've known for ages that I had fertility problems.'

'How long did you and Vince try for?'

Penny heard the tentativeness in Jasmine's

question. They were both working on their relationship, but there were still areas between them that were rarely, if ever, discussed.

'Two years,' Penny finally answered.

One year of serious trying and then a year of endless tests and consultations and a relationship that hadn't been able to take the strain. 'We didn't just break up over that, though,' Penny admitted. 'But it certainly didn't help. I can tell you this much.' She gave a tight smile. 'We'd never have survived IVF. It doesn't exactly bring out the best in you.'

'How are you feeling this time?' Jasmine asked.

'Terrible,' Penny admitted. 'I'm getting hot flashes.'

'Are you serious?'

'I'm completely serious. I'd forgotten that part—you know, at the time you think that you will never forget, but you actually do.'

Jasmine opened her mouth to agree with her

sister and then closed it again as Penny turned around.

Penny knew that Jasmine had been about to admit to the same thing, but for very different reasons—Jasmine's breasts were noticeably larger and she'd had nothing to eat at the airport and had then screwed up her nose when Penny had suggested they get some takeaway for dinner, choosing instead a slow walk on the beach.

Jasmine was pregnant.

Penny just knew.

'I don't need the whole department watching me for signs of a baby bump,' Penny said, though it was the opposite for Penny with her sister. She had been trying so hard to ignore the signs in Jasmine, but more and more it was becoming evident and Penny wished she would just come out and tell her now. 'Or gossiping,' Penny added.

'It wouldn't be like that.'

'Of course it would,' Penny snapped. 'And, of course, they'll all have an opinion on whether I should be doing this, given that I haven't got a partner.' She gave an exasperated sigh. It wasn't a decision she was taking lightly, not in the least. At thirty-four there was no sign of Mr Right on the horizon and with her fertility issues, even if he did come along, it was going to be a struggle to get pregnant.

After many long conversations with the fertility consultant, more and more Penny felt as if time was running out. 'If there's good news at the end of this, I'll tell people, but they don't need to know that I'm trying.'

'But the treatment is so intense. If people only knew…'

Penny didn't let her finish. 'You don't walk into the staffroom and tell them that you've come off the pill and had sex with Jed last night.' When Jasmine laughed, Penny carried on. 'No, you feed the sharks when you're good and ready.' Penny paused, waiting for her sister to open up to her, because even if Penny snapped and snarled a bit she wasn't a shark, but Jasmine changed the subject.

'I can't believe that Mum has finally made it to her cruise.' Jasmine smiled. 'Well, she's made it to her flight.'

'And she'll make it to her cruise.' Penny was firm.

'What if something happens while she's stuck in the middle of the ocean?'

'There's a medical team,' Penny said, but of course that didn't reassure her sister. 'Jasmine, are you going to spend the next month worrying about things that might happen and every imagined scenario while Mum is no doubt having the absolute time of her life?'

'I guess,' Jasmine conceded. 'Though I really did think we were going to lose her.'

'We didn't, though,' Penny broke in.

While Louise Masters's heart attack and emergency admission had been a most difficult time, from there good things had sprung—an urgent reminder for all concerned that you should live your life to the full.

Which was why their mother would soon be sailing around the Mediterranean, why Jasmine had followed her heart and opened up to Penny's then fellow senior registrar Jed, and why Penny was, at this moment, walking along the beach with a face that was bright red and breaking out into a sweat as she experienced yet another wretched hot flash. Not that Jasmine noticed; her mind had moved on to other things.

'What do you think of Ethan?' Jasmine asked for Penny's thoughts on the new consultant, but Penny didn't answer; instead, she suggested a walk in the shallows, much to little Simon's delight. Both holding his hands, they lifted him up between them, swung him over the water, and finally Penny felt herself calm, the heat fading from her face, her racing heart slowing, and then Jasmine asked her again what she thought of Ethan.

'He thinks that he's God's gift.'

'So do a few other people,' Jasmine pointed out, because since Ethan had arrived, a couple of hearts had already been broken. 'He is funny, though.' Jasmine grinned.

'I don't think he's funny at all,' Penny said, but then again she didn't sit in the little huddles at the nurses' station, neither did she wait for the latest breaking news to be announced in the staffroom. Penny loathed gossip and refused to partake in it, though, given it was Jasmine, there was one thing she did divulge. 'He seems to think that he got the job over me.' Penny gave a little smirk. 'He has no idea that I declined to take it.'

'He doesn't know?'

'God, no!' Penny said. 'I would assume he knows that Jed turned it down to take the position at Melbourne Central, but it would be a bit much for him to know that he was actually the third choice.'

'Wouldn't Mr Dean have told him?'

'Mr Dean wouldn't discuss the other applicants

with him—you know what he's like.' Penny
rolled her eyes. Mr Dean had put her through
the wringer over the years—he was incredibly
chauvinistic and had been reluctant to promote
Penny to senior registrar. Penny was quite sure
it was because she was a woman—she'd heard
Mr Dean comment a few times how you trained
women up only for them to get pregnant. Still,
Penny had long since proven herself and, though
Ethan might think otherwise, the consultant's
position had been Penny's. She had chosen not
to take it, deciding it would be too much on top
of going through IVF, and more and more she
was glad she had made that decision.

'Ethan's gorgeous.' Jasmine nudged her. 'He's
so sexy.'

'Jasmine!'

'What? Just because I'm married I'm not supposed to notice just how stunning he is?'

Penny conceded with a shrug. Yes, Ethan
Lewis was stunning. He had thick silky black
hair that seemed always to be just a day away

from needing a good cut and had unusual hazel eyes. He was very tall and broad shouldered and so naturally he stood out. He was also a bit chauvinistic, not that the women seemed to mind.

'The trouble with Ethan,' Penny said, 'is that he knows how gorgeous he is and he uses it unwisely. Someone should stamp "not the settling-down type" on his forehead. It might have helped warn the nurse in CCU who keeps coming down to the department to try and speak to him, and also that physiotherapist.'

Penny frowned as she tried to think of the young woman's name, but gave up. 'And that's just two that I've seen and heard about, and given that I'm the last person to know anything, I'm quite sure there must be a few more.'

'Well, at least he doesn't pretend he's interested in anything more serious,' Jasmine said. 'I was talking to him the other day and I apologised for going on too much about Simon and he just laughed and said he enjoyed hearing it, as it's the closest he'll ever get to having one of his own. He's lovely,' Jasmine sighed. 'You should have a fling with him.'

Jasmine would so love to see her very uptight sister unbend just a little. 'She should, shouldn't she, Simon?' Jasmine said as she picked up her little boy, who was finally starting to tire.

'Don't bring Simon into this.' Penny smiled fondly at her nephew. 'And don't you listen to your mother.'

Simon smiled back. He adored his aunt and he held out his hands for Penny to hold him, which she did. 'You're the cause of all this,' Penny teased, because seeing her sister pregnant and later as a mum had stirred already jumbled feelings in Penny and she desperately wanted a baby of her own.

'You tell Aunty Penny that she *should* listen to me and have some fun before she's ankle deep in nappies and exhausted from lack of sleep.' Jasmine smiled at her son and then turned to her sister. 'Just one last wild fling before you get pregnant!'

'I've never had a wild fling in my life and I'm certainly not about to start now. You've never had IVF, have you?' Penny's voice was wry. 'Believe me, Ethan Lewis and sex and wild flings are the very last thing on my mind right now.' Penny did suddenly laugh, though. 'Could you imagine if I did and then twelve weeks later announced that I'm pregnant?'

'Oh, I would just love to see that.' Jasmine was laughing too at the thought of the confirmed bachelor Ethan Lewis thinking for a moment that he was about to become a father. 'It would kill him!'

CHAPTER TWO

'WHERE THE HELL is X-ray?' Penny snapped at Jasmine the next afternoon, just as she would to anyone—they weren't sisters here and no feelings were spared.

They were struggling to stabilise a patient in congestive heart failure who wasn't responding to the usual treatment regimes. John Douglas had presented to the department struggling to breathe, his heart beating dangerously fast and his lungs overloaded with fluid. It was a common emergency that Penny was more than used to dealing with, but what was compounding the problem was that John was also a renal patient and undergoing regular dialysis at a major city hospital so Penny was trying to sort out the far higher drug doses that were needed in his case.

'I'm just going to lean you forward, John,' Penny said, and listened again to her patient's chest. The oxygen saturation machine was bleeping its alarm. Vanessa, another nurse, returned with John's blood-gas results and it was confirmed to Penny that things were really grim. She had already paged the medics to come down urgently and was now considering putting out a crash call, because even though he hadn't gone into cardiac arrest he was very close.

'Give him another forty milligrams,' Penny called out to Jasmine, though she wasn't cross when Jasmine hesitated. 'He's a renal patient,' Penny explained, 'so he'll need massive doses of diuretics.'

Still, Penny was concerned about the amount of medication she was having to give and was carefully checking the drug guide, wishing the medics would hurry up and get there. She had just decided to put out a crash call when Ethan approached.

'Problem?' Ethan asked, and Penny quickly brought him up to speed.

'He's not responding,' Penny said. 'And neither are the medics to their fast page. I'm going to call the crash team.'

'Hold off for just a moment.' Ethan scanned the drug sheet to see what had been given. He had just come from working a rotation in the major renal unit in a city hospital, so he was familiar with the drug doses required in a case like this and he quickly examined the patient. 'He needs a large bolus.'

Ethan saw Penny's face go bright red as he took over the patient's care. 'Penny, where I worked before…' He didn't really have time to explain things and he wasn't about to compromise patient care by pandering to Penny's fragile ego—she was spitting with rage, Ethan could see it. In fact, he was tempted to lick his finger and put it onto her flaming cheek just so that he could hear the hiss.

'Go ahead,' came Penny's curt response, and

she thrust the patient notes into his hands and walked off quickly.

'Have we ordered a portable chest X-ray?' he asked Jasmine.

'It's supposed to be on its way,' Jasmine answered.

'You're going to be okay, sir.' Ethan listened to his chest and considered calling the crash team himself.

He could see Jasmine was blushing too at her sister's little outburst and was sorely tempted to ask Jasmine just what the hell her sister's problem was, though of course Ethan knew. Well, he wasn't just going to stand back, and if Penny didn't like it, she'd better start getting used to it. Penny Masters was an absolute… Ethan kept the word in his head as he saw the fluid start to gush into the catheter bag. The patient's oxygen saturations started to rise slowly. He was just ordering some more morphine when the radiographer arrived for the chest X-ray, along with a much calmer-looking Penny.

'Thanks for that,' she said, completely unable to look him in the eye. She had fled to her office, which had a small sink in it, and splashed her face with cold water and run her wrists under the tap. Penny would never have left the patient had Ethan not been there, but she had never had a hot flash so severe. She knew that Ethan was less than impressed, especially when, without a further word, he stalked off.

'Are you okay?' Jasmine checked as they waited outside while the patient was being X-rayed, Vanessa staying in with him.

'Of course I'm not.' Rarely for Penny, she was close to tears. 'He thought I was cross at him for making suggestions and that I just walked off in a temper.'

He'd thought exactly that, Jasmine knew. She had seen the roll of his tongue in his cheek and the less than impressed rise of Ethan's brows. 'Penny, if people just knew—'

'What?' Penny interrupted. 'Do you really

think that I'm going to explain to him that I just had a hot flash?'

Penny was mortified—absolutely and completely mortified. The down-regulation medication to stop her own cycle was in full effect, and she had a splitting headache as well, another of the side effects. The headache she could deal with, but for a woman who was usually so able to keep things in check, the rip of heat that had seared through her face and the rapid flutter of her heart in her chest had felt appalling. She had hardly been able to breathe in there but she had absolutely no intention of telling Ethan Lewis why. 'Do you really think that Neanderthal would be understanding?'

'Neanderthal?' Jasmine grinned in delight at her sister's choice of word.

'Just leave it,' Penny snapped.

Ethan didn't leave it, though.

Before heading for home, he passed her office, where Penny sat busily writing up her notes. She was sitting very straight, like some schoolmarm,

Ethan thought as he knocked a couple of times on her open door.

In fact, it was rather like walking into the headmistress's office as those cold blue eyes lifted to his and gave him a very stern stare.

'What time are you on till?' Ethan asked.

'Midnight,' Penny answered—she knew that he hadn't just popped in for a chat.

'How is Mr Douglas doing now?'

'He's a lot better, but the medics are still stabilising him and then he'll be transferred so he can have his dialysis.' She wished he would just leave; she really didn't want to discuss what had taken place. 'Thank you for your help with him.'

'It didn't feel very welcome.' Ethan waited a moment, but Penny said nothing, just turned her attention back to her notes and, no, he would not just leave it. 'What the hell happened back there, Penny?'

'I don't know what you're talking about.'

'I think that you do,' came Ethan's swift retort. 'If there is an issue then it's time that we discussed it.'

'There is no issue.'

Ethan begged to differ. She was the most difficult woman that he had ever met and he'd met a lot of women! Yes, she was a fantastic doctor. Ethan had no qualms there, and in fact he was quietly surprised, having seen her work, that she hadn't been given the consultant's position. He could well understand how angry she must be, but somehow they had to work together and if she was going to storm off every time he stepped in on a consultation, something had to be said. 'We have to work together, Penny.'

'I'm aware of that.'

'Which means that at times we'll disagree.'

'I'm aware of that too.' Her face was starting to burn again, but from embarrassment this time. 'Look, thank you for stepping in with Mr Douglas, it was much appreciated. I'm not as familiar as I would like to be with renal patients so I'm very pleased that you were there. We do seem to have our wires crossed, though.' She gave tight smile. 'I wasn't cross or upset.' She saw his incredulous look.

'You walked off.'

Penny said nothing, just stared at this huge, very masculine man. She didn't know how to tell him and she didn't really want to try, except her silence invited him to continue speaking.

'I wasn't trying to take over. You seem to have formed an opinion that I'm—'

'Formed an opinion?' Penny stopped him right there. 'I'm actually a bit busy in my life right now. I haven't had time to think, let alone form an opinion of you.'

His lips twitched almost into a smile at her not-too-subtle putdown. 'Oh, but I think that you have,' Ethan said, and there and then he took the gloves off. He'd tried niceness, he'd tried politeness, he'd accepted that the situation might be a little difficult for her, but at the end of the day Penny needed to get over it and accept that he had been given the job. 'Do you know what,

Penny? I'm starting to form an opinion of you, and your behaviour this afternoon is leading me to think it might be the right one.'

'Whatever!' Penny hadn't got this far in her career on charm. To do her job you needed to be tough and she certainly wasn't there to make friends. 'You carry right on forming your opinion of me and, while you do, I'll get back to my patients.' Penny stood. 'Or is there anything else you want to discuss?'

'Nothing that won't keep.'

She brushed past him and he was terribly tempted to catch her as she walked past, to turn her round and just have the row that was so clearly needed. Perhaps it was wiser to just let it go, Ethan thought, letting out a rare angry breath as he heard her heels clip down the corridor, but he turned at the sound of Lisa's voice. 'There he is.'

'Kate?' Ethan smiled when he saw that Lisa was with his sister, wondered, albeit briefly, what on earth she was doing at his workplace, and then properly read her face. 'One of the kids...'

'The kids are fine, Ethan.' She took a breath and he knew what was coming. 'It's Phil—we need to get to the hospital.' And still his brain tried to process things kindly. He waited for her to smile, to hold up crossed fingers and to say 'this is it,' that a heart had been found for their cousin, but she just looked at him. 'Carl's watching the kids. We need to hurry and get there.'

No, it would seem that Phil wasn't going to get that heart.

Ethan was glad that Kate hadn't told him by phone, realised that had he not stopped to talk to Penny he could have been sitting in his car, stuck on the packed Beach Road and finding out that Phil was about to die.

'I'll meet you there.' He was already heading to his office to grab his car keys but Kate shook her head. She knew how close Ethan and Phil were.

'I'll drive.'

It was just as well that she did, because the rush-hour traffic didn't care that there was somewhere they needed to be. Ethan could feel his temper building as they inched towards the hospital, could sense the mounting urgency, especially when his mother called to see how far away they were.

'A couple of minutes,' Ethan said.

'Get here,' came his mother's response.

They were pulling into Melbourne Central and again Ethan was very glad that Kate had been driving. He was grateful that there was no competition in the grief stakes between him and his twin—she knew that he and Phil were like brothers. Kate dropped him off at the main entrance and then went to find a place to park the car as Ethan ran through the hospital building, desperate to get to his cousin in time, still holding a small flame of hope that something could yet be done.

It was extinguished even before he got to Phil's room.

Because standing outside was Phil's ex-wife, Gina, and unless he was dying she'd never be there otherwise. She'd be sitting outside in the canteen as she usually did when she brought Justin in to visit. It had been a wretched divorce and Phil's parents hadn't exactly been kind in their summing up of Gina—and not just behind her back. There had been some terrible arguments too.

'Gina,' he said, but she just flashed him a look that said he was a part of the Lewis family and could he please just stay back.

'I'm here for Justin,' Gina said, and Ethan nodded and went in the room. His eyes didn't first go to Phil but to Justin. Ethan could see the bewilderment and fear on the little boy's face as Vera and Jack, Phil's parents, told him to be brave. Ethan felt his head tighten, wanted to tell them to stop, but then his eyes moved to the bed and to his cousin and there wasn't even time to say to Phil all he wanted to.

It was all over by the time Kate arrived.

CHAPTER THREE

PENNY PARKED HER car and took a couple of moments to sort out her make-up and hair. She wondered, not for the first time, how she was going to get through this. It was eight a.m. and she had just come from having a blood test and vaginal ultrasound. If the results were as expected, she would be starting her injections this evening.

She collected her handbag and the little cool bag holding the medication and told herself that lots of women worked while they went through this.

And she told herself something else, something she had decided last night—at the very first opportunity she would apologise properly to Ethan. Penny had come up with a plan. She wouldn't tell him everything, just explain to him that she was on some medication and that yesterday she hadn't felt very well. If he probed, she might hint that it was a feminine issue.

Her lips twitched into a smile as she pictured Ethan's reaction—that would soon silence him.

Walking towards Emergency, Penny saw a dark blue car pull up in the entrance bay, where the ambulances did, and she watched as a security guard walked towards it to warn the occupants that they couldn't park there.

Except the woman wasn't parking her car.

Instead, she was dropping Ethan Lewis off.

Penny tried not to look as they shared a brief embrace and then a thoroughly seedy-looking Ethan climbed out. He was unshaven and unkempt, dressed in yesterday's rumpled scrubs. She tried to turn her attention away from him, but her gaze went straight to the car he had just come from. And it was then that Penny felt it— the red-hot poker that jabbed into her stomach as she glanced at the woman, a red-hot poker that temporarily nudged aside her loudly ticking biological clock. And at six minutes past eight and a few months later than most women at Peninsula Hospital, Penny realised that Ethan Lewis really was an incredibly sexy man and it wasn't a hot flash that was causing her to blush as they walked into the department together.

'Ethan.' She tried to keep to the script she had planned. 'I was wondering if I could speak to you about yesterday. I realise that I—'

'Just leave it.' He completely dismissed her, so much so that he strode ahead of her and into the male changing rooms.

Charming!

Ethan ignored her all day and Penny decided that she wasn't about to try apologising again.

She took her lunch break in her office, waiting for the IVF nurse to ring, which she did right on time. Penny took a deep breath as she found out that, as expected, she was to start her injections that evening, which meant she needed to call Jasmine.

'I'm on till six,' Penny said. 'I don't think I'll be able to get away early.'

'Penny, when do you ever get away early? It's not a problem, I'll come and give it to you at work, but Jed won't be home so I'll have to bring Simon in.'

Penny grimaced. She did not want to make a fool of herself in front of her nephew as it would terrify him. Simon, like his mother, was very sensitive. Still, there was no choice.

There really wasn't time to worry about her upcoming jab. The department was busy enough to keep her mind off it and she smiled when she saw her next patient, an eight-week-old named Daniel.

'He's had a bit of a cold,' Laura, the mother, explained. 'I took him to my doctor yesterday and he said that he didn't have a temperature and his chest sounded fine. I've been putting drops up his nose to help with feeding,' Laura continued. 'But this afternoon I came in from putting out the washing and went to check on him and he was pale, really pale, and he'd been sick. I know he's fine now...'

He seemed fine and Penny examined Daniel thoroughly, but apart from a cold and a low-grade temperature there was nothing remarkable to find.

'Has he been coughing?'

'A bit,' Laura said, as Penny listened carefully to his chest, but apart from a couple of crackles it was clear.

Still, Penny was concerned and it did sound as if he might have had an apnoeic episode so she decided to ring the paediatricians, who were very busy on the ward.

'They're going to be a while,' Penny explained to the mum. 'I'm going to take some bloods and do some swabs, so hopefully we'll have some results back by the time they get down here. And I'll order a chest X-ray.'

To show that she wasn't, in fact, too up herself to value Ethan's opinion, late in the afternoon when she was concerned about the baby and the paediatricians weren't anywhere around, instead of speaking with Mr Dean, Penny decided that she would ask Ethan.

He barely looked up from the form he was filling out when Penny asked if she could have a word.

'Sure.'

'I've got an eight-week-old I'm concerned about.' He glanced up. 'Mum found him very pale in his cot after his nap and he'd vomited, but he picked up well. He's had a cold, struggling to feed, he's a bit sniffly, just…' She moved her hand to show she was wavering. 'His chest is clear, and he's got a small cough, which is un-remarkable. I've done some swabs and some bloods.'

'What did paeds say?' Ethan asked.

'They'll come down when they can, but they're busy and they're going to be ages,' Penny said. 'Mum just wants to take him home now that he's had the tests and wait to get the results, but I'm not sure.'

Ethan came and though he had been scowling at Penny, he was lovely with the mum. He carefully checked the infant, who was bright and alert and just hungry. Penny put some saline drops in his nose and they watched as the baby latched on and started to feed happily, but just as Ethan was about to go, Daniel spluttered and broke into a coughing fit. As he came off the breast Ethan took him and held him and Penny watched, the diagnosis becoming more and more evident as he broke into a prolonged paroxysmal cough and then struggled to inhale and then cough again. Ethan was holding him up and tapping his back as Penny turned on the suction, but thankfully it wasn't needed.

'He wasn't doing that.' Laura was beside herself, watching her son. 'He's just had a little cough.'

'That might have been what happened this afternoon,' Penny said, 'when you found him in his cot.' She had to explain to the mother that it would seem her baby had whooping cough.

'He's not making any noises, though.'

'People, especially babies, don't always, but he's struggling to get air in during the coughing attack,' Penny explained. 'It's not evident straight away but he's moved into the coughing stage now.' She looked at the baby Ethan was holding—he had stopped coughing and was again desperate to be fed. 'I'm going to call the paediatricians...'

'Can I feed him?'

'I'll watch him feed while you go and call Paeds,' Ethan said to Penny, handing the crying baby back to his mum. 'Wait one moment before you feed him.' He stepped out with Penny. 'He's to be transferred. I know he seems fine at the moment but, given his age, he needs to be somewhere with PICU.'

'I know.' Penny nodded.

'Can you get Lisa to come in and watch him feed? I'll stay in for now.'

Penny nodded. The coughing episodes were scary at best and someone calm and experienced needed to be in with the mum to help deal with them. 'I've never actually seen whooping cough,' Penny said to Lisa.

'I've had it,' Lisa said. 'Hundred-day cough they call it and I know why. Poor baby and poor mum having to watch him. I'll go and relieve Ethan.'

Penny spoke again to the paediatrician and started the baby on antibiotics, but really there was no treatment that could stop the coughing attacks and, as Ethan had said, given his tender age, he really did need to be somewhere with paediatric intensive care facilities in case he suddenly deteriorated.

'They're going to come down and see him just as soon as they can,' Penny said when Ethan came out. 'I'll go and let mum know.'

'She's in for a tough time,' Ethan said. 'Are you immunised?'

'All up to date,' Penny said, because though she was terrified of injections, before embarking on IVF she had *made* herself get all her immunisations up to date and poor Jasmine had been the one who'd had to do them. Still, it was worth it, Penny realised, for days such as this.

'Right.' Ethan glanced at his watch. 'I'm going home.'

'See you tomorrow,' Penny said, but Ethan shook his head.

'I'm on days off now.'

'Enjoy them.'

He didn't answer. In fact, since her attempt to apologise, unless it was about a patient, Ethan had said nothing at all to her and she felt like poking her tongue out at his back as he and his bad mood walked off together.

Maybe it was just as well he was on days off. Hopefully by the time he was back they could put yesterday's incident behind them and start again.

And she'd hopefully be finished with the hot flashes by then.

As predicted, there wasn't a hope of her getting away at six, but when it neared, Penny told

Lisa she was taking a short break and, seeing Jasmine walking down the corridor with Simon in his stroller, the moment she had been silently dreading all day was finally here.

'I don't want Simon seeing me upset.' Penny was starting to panic. 'It could make him as terrified of needles as I am.'

'There'll be someone in the staffroom who can watch him for five minutes,' Jasmine said. 'You go on and get everything ready and I'll come in.' They both knew it wasn't a question of Penny being brave because her nephew was there—it was the one thing, apart from her fertility, that Penny couldn't control, and her response to injections was varied and unpredictable.

'Vanessa's watching him,' Jasmine said when she came into the office a few minutes later.

'I don't know if I can do this again,' Penny said. Her hand was shaking as she checked the doses the IVF nurse had given her.

'In a couple of moments you'll be one evening down.'

'With God knows how many more to go,' Penny said. She took a deep breath and undid her skirt. 'Just do it.'

She closed her eyes but could not stop shaking as Jasmine walked over. She had hoped so much that things would be different this time, but she was crying again, just as she had that morning at her blood test, and she was very glad that Simon wasn't there to see his aunt make an absolute fool of herself.

'It's done.' Jasmine massaged in the medication. 'You're done for the day.'

'It's ridiculous,' Penny whimpered. 'I've given so many injections today, I've taken blood from an eight-week-old...'

'Don't worry about it,' Jasmine said. 'You're actually better than you used to be.'

'Really?'

'A bit,' Jasmine lied. 'How are the hot flashes?'

'Only two today.'

'How's Ethan been?' Jasmine asked as Penny tucked herself in.

'Horrible,' Penny said. 'He's still sulking about yesterday. I tried to apologise but he wasn't having any of it. There's not much more that I can do.'

But even if she shrugged it off to her sister, Penny was rattled because, yes, she had wanted to put it behind them, had wanted to start again, and, no, she didn't want to but she felt the tiniest bit attracted to him.

CHAPTER FOUR

ETHAN HAD LONG known that his cousin might die but on the eve of the funeral he couldn't really acknowledge that Phil had.

Kate kept ringing and asking him to come over, except he didn't want to talk about it, not even with those closest to him. Ethan had been dreading the funeral, had found himself starting to tear up when he'd asked Gordon to cover for him for the day, though he had kept the details minimal. Then Gordon rang to tell Ethan that he was up in Maternity as his wife, Hilary, had gone into early labour so he wouldn't be able to cover Ethan's shift after all.

'Someone else should be able to cover you, though.'

'It's fine, Gordon,' Ethan said. 'I'll sort something out, you just do what you have to.' He wished him good luck and then looked at the roster. There were several doctors he could change with, he and Penny were on till six today, but tomorrow…

As she walked past he called over to her. Penny was perhaps not his first choice to ask, but it was a pretty straight swap.

'Can I ask a favour?'

Please, don't, Penny thought as she saw him looking at the roster because, in her impossible schedule, for the next couple of weeks there really was no room for manoeuvre, not that Ethan would know that.

'Tomorrow I'm on from nine till six and you're twelve till nine—is there any chance we can swap?' She just blinked. 'Though I might not get in till one.'

'I can't swap tomorrow, Ethan.' She couldn't. Not only did she have an ultrasound and blood test booked for tomorrow, she had a meeting with the specialist at nine.

'I've got to attend a funeral,' Ethan pushed, but didn't go into detail, didn't tell her that this was personal, he simply couldn't. 'Gordon was supposed to be covering for me, but his wife has gone into labour—premature labour,' he added.

Penny hesitated; she knew she couldn't say no.

Except she couldn't say yes either, she simply could not miss her blood test—it was as essential as that.

She'd ring the IVF nurse, Penny decided, see if she could fiddle around her appointment, but for now, till she had, she'd have to stand firm.

'Is there anybody else you can ask?'

'A few.'

'Well, see if they can help and if not, let me know.'

If she occasionally smiled, Ethan thought, she would actually be exceptionally attractive, but even then, with her terse attitude and unfeeling ways, Penny could never be considered beautiful. A black smile spread across his lips. She really was the limit and instead of leaving it there, Ethan found that he couldn't. 'What is your problem, Penny?'

'Problem?' Penny frowned. 'I don't have a problem. I simply can't come in early tomorrow, that's all.'

'It was the same when I asked you to come in for a few hours the other day.'

'So that you could go to a football match.' Penny stared back coolly, looking into his angry eyes and surprisingly tempted to tell him that she had a vaginal ultrasound and a blood test booked for ten past eight tomorrow, just so that she could watch him squirm. 'I'm sorry, Ethan, I have things on. I'm not able to simply change my schedule at a moment's notice. If you can check with the others...'

'Like it or not,' Ethan said, 'there has to be a senior staff member on at all times, and that sometimes means making last-minute changes to the roster.'

'I'm aware of that,' Penny responded.

'Yet you don't...' He watched two spots of

colour rising on her cheeks, and then she turned abruptly to go, but Ethan refused to leave it there. 'You're going to have to be more flexible.'

Her back was to him and he watched as Penny stilled, her shoulders stiffened and she slowly turned around. 'Excuse me?'

'In the coming days you're going to have to be more flexible—Gordon will need some time after all.'

'If Gordon's wife having a baby leaves us short-staffed then it might be prudent to look at getting a locum because—and I am warning you now—I am not going to be dropping everything and coming into work and leaving here late and changing shifts at the last moment to accommodate Gordon, his wife and their baby.'

Penny was angry now and with good reason—part of her mandatory counselling before she'd commenced IVF had addressed problems such as this. Timing was important. These weeks were incredibly intense and to keep it from becoming a staffroom topic of conversation Penny had worked out her appointments very carefully around her work schedule. And now Hilary had gone into labour and she was supposed to juggle everything.

Well, Penny was doing this for *her* baby.

'You're such a team player,' Ethan said.

'Oh, but I'm not,' Penny responded. 'Ask anyone.'

'I don't need to ask, I'd say it's already common knowledge.' It was——Penny was the ice queen. He'd heard it from many and had seen it for himself, but she hadn't finished yet, pulling Ethan up on a very pertinent point.

'You're talking as if Hilary is about to deliver a micro-prem when, in fact, she's actually thirty-five weeks' gestation.' Ethan at that point actually had to suppress a smile, because she had well and truly caught him out. When he'd said premature labour he had been appealing or rather searching for the softer side to Penny, but he was fast realising that she simply didn't have one. 'I don't respond to bells and whistles,

Ethan. Give me a real drama and I'll deal with it accordingly.' She walked off and Ethan watched.

She was absolutely immaculate. Her straight blonde hair was tied low at the back of her neck. Her sheer cream blouse looked as if it had come straight off a mannequin at an expensive boutique and her charcoal-grey skirt was perfectly cut to show a very trim figure. If she had been just a few inches taller she could be walking down a runway instead of the corridor of the emergency department.

'What do you respond to, Penny?' The words were out of Ethan's mouth before his brain had even processed them, and how he wished, the moment they were uttered, that he could take them back.

He was more than aware of the not-so-slight sexual undertone to them, and Ethan half expected her to turn on her low heels and march back to give him a sharp piece of her mind, or perhaps to head straight to Mr Dean's office, but what happened next came as a complete surprise.

Ethan watched as Penny threw her head back and laughed and then glanced over her shoulder at him. He saw not the glitter of ice in those cold blue eyes but something far more fetching. And her mouth was parted in a slightly mocking yet somehow mischievous smile as she answered him. 'That's for me to know!'

Ethan found himself smiling back, a proper smile this time. He almost called out that he was looking forward to finding out but then he checked himself, the smile fading, and he turned back to the roster he had been viewing before Penny had come along, and wondered what the hell had just happened. She had been completely immutable with the roster, thoroughly unfriendly and yet somehow it had ended in a smile.

A flirtatious one at that.

Ethan had no trouble with flirting—he was an expert at it, in fact. He had just never expected to find himself going there with Penny, but more to the point, Ethan thought darkly, he still didn't have anyone to cover him for the funeral.

'Not now!' Penny said a few moments later when Jasmine knocked on her office door as she came in to start her late shift. Penny was seriously rattled by the small confrontation she'd had with Ethan and wanted a few moments alone to process things and to ring the IVF nurse to see if she could possibly swap. More unsettling than that, though, was the flutter in her throat and the blush on her cheeks at her response to him. Her face still burnt red even as she tried to put off her sister from coming in, but Jasmine wanted a quick word.

'It won't take a second—I'm just letting you know that Mum rang this morning from a satellite phone.'

'Where is she?' Penny smiled and it was genuine. She was thrilled to hear from her mum.

'Heading for Mykonos,' Jasmine said, and Penny groaned her envy.

'I'm sure that I don't need to ask if she's having a good time.'

'Completely loving it,' Jasmine said. 'She said that she should've done this years ago and… don't fall off your chair, but I think she might have met someone.'

'You mean a man?' Penny blinked in surprise. 'I don't know what to say…I don't know what to think.'

'I know.' Jasmine smiled. 'I can't imagine Mum with anyone.'

Louise Masters had been single since the day her husband had left. A very volatile marriage had made Louise swear off men and instead she had focused heavily on her career and had done her best to instil the same very independent, somewhat bitter values into her daughters.

'Anyway,' Jasmine continued, 'we didn't talk for long. I've no idea how much it would have cost her to call. She just wanted to send her love and to find out how you were getting on. I told her that you were doing fine.' Jasmine hesitated.

She'd heard a few whispers, knew that Penny was putting noses out of joint everywhere, which wasn't unusual. Penny was known for being tough, it was just a lot more concentrated at the moment. '*Are* you doing fine, though?'

'Not really,' Penny admitted. 'Actually, Jasmine, I think you're right, I might have to let a few people at work know. It's proving impossible. I've just had an argument with Ethan— he needs me to come in early tomorrow so that he can go to a funeral. God.' Penny buried her face in her hands. 'Imagine saying no to that— it's a funeral!'

'Penny, it was a football match a couple of weeks ago that Ethan asked you to cover him for.' Jasmine was indignant on her sister's behalf. 'And Mr Dean has a corporate golf day on Thursday and Rex is getting a divorce. The fact is that this place needs more doctors, but they still won't employ another one.'

'A funeral, though.' Penny groaned.

'Penny, you go to more funerals than anyone

I know.' It was true. Of course they couldn't attend the funeral of every patient who died, but Penny's black outfits were taken for a trip to the dry cleaner's more than most. 'You *have* to keep the next few weeks clear.' Jasmine was firm. She knew how hard this was for Penny and just how hard her sister worked. 'And I do think you should let your colleagues know. Not everyone, but if you told Lisa…'

'How can Lisa help with the doctors' roster?'

'Well, just tell Ethan or Mr Dean…' Her voice trailed off.

'It's hopeless, isn't it?' Mr Dean wasn't going to be exactly thrilled to find out that his senior registrar was trying to get pregnant—it was the reason he had hesitated to promote her a few years ago—of that Penny was sure.

'Penny, you can't come in early tomorrow. You can't miss a blood test, it determines the whole day's treatment.'

'I know. I just really thought I could handle working and doing this. I thought that it might be easier the second time around, that I'd know more what to expect, that I'd at least be used to the needles.'

'Penny.' Jasmine sat on the edge of her sister's desk. 'I think you are going to have to face the fact that you are never going to get over your fear of needles.'

'I'm an emergency registrar!'

'With one weakness.' Jasmine gave a sympathetic smile. 'It's just a horrible weakness to have when you're going through IVF.'

'I made a right fool of myself this morning at my blood test.' Penny shuddered at the memory. 'It took two of them, one to hold me and one to take the blood. I was crying and carrying on like a two-year-old!'

'Then it's just as well that you're not having your IVF treatment here.'

Penny blanched at the very thought of that happening. Even if Peninsula Hospital offered IVF, which they didn't, Penny wouldn't take it. Oh, for the convenience, it would be wonderful to just pop upstairs for the endless blood tests, injections and scans that were part of the tumultuous ride she was on, but not so convenient would be to have your colleagues see you a shivering, terrified mess. She was bad enough at the best of times, but right now, tired and with her hormones all over the place, it was the worst of times.

'Do you have to work?' Jasmine asked gently.

'I took time off last time,' Penny said. 'And I had all that time off when Mum came out of hospital. I'd actually like to have some annual leave up my sleeve if I ever do get pregnant.'

'You will.' Jasmine slipped off the desk and gave her sister a hug, but it wasn't returned. Penny wasn't particularly touchy-feely. 'You're going to get your baby.'

'Easy for you to say.' Penny tried to keep the bitterness out of her voice. She loved Simon very much, but he had been an accident. Just one mistake had seen Jasmine pregnant. Yes, Jasmine had had a terrible time with a horrible husband

and later as a single mum before she'd married Jed. But now, just a few months into her marriage, she was pregnant, although she hadn't told Penny.

Penny felt her sister's arms around her tense shoulders and it was time to face the white elephant in the room before it came between them.

'When are you going to tell me, Jasmine?' There was a long stretch of silence. 'You're pregnant, aren't you?'

'Penny, I...'

Penny heard the discomfort in her sister's voice and forced a smile before turning her face back to Jasmine. 'How many weeks?'

'Fourteen.' Jasmine flushed.

'Have you told Mum?'

'Not yet. We haven't said anything to anyone yet. I wanted to tell you first but I just didn't know how.' Jasmine's eyes were same blue as her sister's and they filled with tears. 'You were so upset when your last IVF attempt failed and then you've been building up for this one. I know how hard it is for you right now, and to find out my news right in the middle of an IVF treatment cycle, well, I know...'

Except Jasmine didn't know, Penny thought, though at least she tried to understand.

Penny took a deep breath. 'Even if it isn't happening easily for me, it doesn't mean that I can't be pleased for you.'

'You're sure?'

'Of course I am. I know I wasn't the best sister and aunt to Simon at first, but I've told you why. I was jealous when you were pregnant with Simon, but it's different now—I'm honestly pleased for you and Jed.' Penny gave a wry smile. 'And, of course, terribly, terribly jealous.'

'I know.' Jasmine smiled back. 'I'm so glad that we can be more honest with each other now.'

'We can be,' Penny said. 'Which means you won't be offended if I tell you I really need five minutes alone right now.'

'Sure.'

Penny waited till the door was closed and then put her head back in her hands.

Fourteen weeks.

She just sat there, a hormonal jumble of conflict.

She was pleased for her sister.

No, she wasn't!

She was jealous, jealous, jealous, and now she felt guilty for feeling so jealous, yet she was pleased for her sister too.

Oh, hell!

Penny really had forgotten just how awful the treatment made her feel. It was far worse than feeling premenstrual. The last time had been bad enough but she had gone through it at home, concentrating solely on her appointments.

Trying to work through it was unbearable.

And then she remembered her confrontation with Ethan—the reason she had come to the office in the first place—and reached for her phone and rang the IVF nurse to explain her problem. 'I'm booked in for ten past eight,' Penny said. 'I was wondering if I could come in on the early round. And also if, instead of my appointment,

I could have a phone consultation with the specialist.' There was a bit of a tart pause, which Penny took as a warning. You had to be fully on board, she had been told this on many occasions, and she tried so hard to be.

Except she was also expected to be fully on board at work.

'There's a spot at six-twenty a.m.,' the nurse said, and an already exhausted Penny took it. She headed out of the office and back through to the department to catch up with Ethan and to show him what a *team player* she could be, but he was stuck with a baby who had suspicious injuries and later interviewing the parents. Oh, well, Penny thought, it would keep for later. He might already have someone else. Of course, Penny got caught up with work of her own and at the end of a very long shift, with a needle to look forward to, Penny wasn't in the happiest of moods when, just to cap it all off, Gordon came into the department with a huge smile on his face.

'It's a boy!'

'How lovely!' Penny offered her congratulations and Ethan came over and did the same, and they headed over to the nurses' station and stood while Gordon sat showing the many, many photos he had taken on his phone of his gorgeous new son.

'He's doing really well,' Gordon enthused. 'Though they will probably keep him in the nursery for a few days, given that he's a bit small, but we should get him home soon. Hilary's a paediatrician after all.' He gave a tired yawn. 'It's been a long day—do you want to join me in celebrating? Hilary is catching up on some sleep. I thought we could go and have a drink before I head back up there.'

'I'd love to,' Penny said as her phone alarm buzzed in her pocket to remind her that it was injection time. 'But I'm afraid that I can't right now.' She didn't dash straight off, though, and looked at a couple more photos. 'How is Hilary doing?'

'Really well,' Gordon said. 'She's a bit disappointed, of course, but she'll soon come round.'

'Disappointed?' Penny looked at an image of the tiny but, oh, so healthy baby.

'She really wanted a girl this time. Which I guess is understandable after three sons.'

'Didn't you find out what you were having?' Ethan asked Gordon, but Penny wasn't really listening. She could feel the incessant buzz from a phone in her pocket and she needed to go.

'Congratulations again!' Penny said to Gordon. 'But now you'll have to excuse me. Tell Hilary that I shall come up and visit her soon.'

A bit disappointed.

The words buzzed in Penny's ears as she walked around her office. She was being hypersensitive, Penny told herself. It was just that it seemed so easy for everyone else at the moment. Maybe if she had three sons she'd be disappointed too at not getting a girl, except she couldn't imagine it. Worse, she couldn't imagine having three babies—it was hard enough trying to get one.

And then she thought about the baby that Ethan had been looking after that afternoon and all the social workers and police that had been involved, and it just didn't seem fair that some people who had babies didn't even seem to want them.

'Hi, there.' Jasmine was waiting for Penny in her office. She had everything set up for the tiny injection that really should only take a minute, except Penny needed to be talked down from the ceiling each and every time. Penny hated the weakness. She'd had hypnosis and even counselling in a bid to overcome it, not that it changed a single thing. Every needle that went into her had her shaking with fear and this evening was no exception. If anything, this evening she was worse.

'I can't do this today,' Penny said as she closed the office door and let out a shaky breath. 'I'm honestly not just saying it this time, Jasmine. I'm really not up to it.'

'Penny.' Jasmine was very patient; she was more than used to this. 'You know that you can't miss one injection.'

'I don't think I want to do the treatment anymore.' Penny just said it. 'I can't keep going on like this. I'm snapping at everyone, I'm in tears all the time.'

'The same as you were last time,' Jasmine said.

'I was going to ring in sick tomorrow, or ask Mr Dean if I could take annual leave, but now with Gordon's wife having the baby...' Penny closed her eyes at the impossibility of it all. 'I don't want the injection.'

'You're *going* to finish this course.'

'And what if it doesn't work?'

'Then you'll have a proper break before you put yourself through this again,' Jasmine said firmly. 'It's no wonder that you're teary and exhausted. Let's just get this needle over and done with and then we'll talk.'

And she would have, except there was a sharp knock on Penny's door.

'Penny?' There was no mistaking Ethan's low voice, but Penny didn't answer. She'd forgotten to lock it and when he knocked again, it was so impatient that Penny wouldn't put it past him to simply walk in.

'What?' Penny asked angrily when she opened the door just a fraction.

'I was wondering if you could change your mind and come out for a drink with Gordon and I. There is no one else around to ask and Rex needs to stay here.'

'I can't,' Penny said. 'I've got the case review to prepare for.'

'One drink,' Ethan said. Surely she could manage one quick drink. 'Come on, Penny, I'm asking for some help here. I'm really not in the mood to go out celebrating tonight and I don't know how to do the baby talk thing.'

'Oh, and because I'm a woman, I do?'

'God, you just don't let up, do you?' Ethan snapped. 'I was just asking for some backup. It would be nice to do the right thing by the guy, the sociable thing. His wife's just had a baby, it's right to take him out.'

'It's right that the consultant takes him out!' Penny retorted sharply. 'I'm not a consultant, which means I get to go home and sign off from this place occasionally, and I'm signing off now. Good night, Ethan!'

Penny closed the door on him and promptly burst into tears. And because Jasmine knew her well, or rather better than anyone else knew Penny, she didn't try to comfort her at first. Instead, she undid her sister's skirt as Penny stood there and sobbed. Jasmine looked at her bruised stomach and, finding a suitable spot, swabbed her skin and then stuck in the needle. Penny continued to sob and then, having disposed of the needle, Jasmine went over and gave her sister a hug.

'It's done.'

'It's not just that,' Penny said.

'I know.'

'I made a right fool of myself just then. Ethan

thinks that I'm jealous because I didn't get the job. I know that's what he's been thinking and I've just gone and proved it to him.'

'You're not jealous, though, Penny.' Jasmine tried to get her sister to see reason. 'He doesn't know what's going on. You turned down the job so that you could concentrate on your IVF.'

'No! I turned down the consultant's position so that I could have a baby.' Penny gulped. 'But the way things are going, I don't think that I'm going to get one.'

CHAPTER FIVE

ETHAN PAID THE taxi and let himself into his apartment.

A celebratory drink on an empty stomach, the way he was feeling right now, possibly hadn't been the best idea and it hadn't been just the one.

Given it had only been him with Gordon, he hadn't exactly been able to get up and leave after one, so instead he'd had to sit there and listen as Gordon had gone into spectacular detail about his day, or rather his wife's day.

Ethan had been hoping that now that the baby had been born, Gordon would come back to work.

He'd had no idea how it all worked.

As it turned out, Gordon was now on paternity leave and would be juggling toddler twins and a six-year-old's school run.

'Not a problem,' he had said to Gordon.

It was, though, a huge one.

Ethan had gone through everyone to cover for him in the morning and the only person who might possibly have been able to help had an *appointment*.

Well, Ethan had his cousin's funeral to attend.

He'd been dreading it, but he would far rather be there than not.

He would love to just ring in sick tomorrow, to let someone else sort it out, to just sign off on the place, as Penny had tonight.

Still, he had expected more from her.

She was senior too.

Ethan loaded some toast into the toaster and some tinned spaghetti into the microwave and tried not to think about Justin and how he'd be feeling tonight. Though, he consoled himself, Gina would surely be handling things better than his own mother had, given they had broken up a couple of years ago.

He couldn't not be there tomorrow and not just

for appearances' sake—Ethan wanted to see for himself that Justin was okay.

Ethan thought about Phil and the black game they'd played and, sorry, mate, he said to his cousin, because even if he didn't fancy Penny, he was going to have to play the sympathy card.

He was scrolling through his phone to find her number when it rang.

'Ethan?' He didn't answer her straight away; instead, he frowned at the sound of her voice. 'It's Penny. Penny Masters from work.'

'Hi, Penny.'

'I'm sorry to call you so late. I meant to tell you before I left for home—it just slipped my mind. I changed my appointment. I can get into work by nine tomorrow, if you still need me to.'

'I do.' The words just jumped out of him. 'Thank you.' Ethan closed his eyes in relief and it took a second to realise that she was still talking.

'I'd also like to apologise for my words before.' She sounded very prim and formal. 'I really wasn't in a position to go out tonight, but I didn't explain myself very well.'

Penny had explained things perfectly, Ethan thought privately, but he was so relieved that he would be able to get the funeral tomorrow that he let go the chance for a little barb, and instead he was nice. 'I don't blame you in the least for not wanting to come out tonight.' Relief, mixed with just a little bit too much champagne, had him speaking honestly. 'I really don't think that I'm going to be able to look Hilary in the eye when I go and visit her.'

'Too much detail?' He *heard* her smile.

'Far, far too much.'

'That's Gordon for you. He's very...' Penny really didn't know how to describe him.

'In tune?' Ethan suggested.

'Something like that.'

'I felt as if I was listening to him describe *his* labour,' Ethan said, and was rewarded by the sound of her laugh. 'Hold on a second.' The microwave was pinging and he pressed Stop on the microwave rather than ending the call, not that he thought about it. 'Look, thanks a lot for tomorrow. I hope it wasn't too much trouble.'

'It was!' Penny said, which had him frowning but sort of smiling too. 'Don't rush back.'

'I'll be back by one.' Ethan really didn't want to stand around chatting and drinking and talking about Phil in the past tense. He would be glad of the chance to slip away and just bury himself in work.

'Whose funeral is it?' Penny asked, and not gently, assuming, because he was fine to dash off from the funeral by one, that it was a patient from work and her mind was sort of scanning the admissions from the previous week as to who it might be, when his voice broke in.

'My cousin's.'

Penny closed her eyes, guilty and horrified too, because she'd been so upset tonight she had almost forgotten to ring him. 'You should have told me that! Ethan, I assumed it was a patient. You should have told me that it was personal.'

'I was just about to call you and do that,' Ethan admitted.

'Is that why you've been so…?' Penny's voice trailed off.

'That's fine, coming from you,' Ethan said, but it actually came out rather nicely and Penny found herself smiling into the phone as he continued. 'Yes, it's been a tough few days.'

'How old?'

'My age,' Ethan said. 'Thirty-six.'

'Was it expected?'

'Sort of,' Ethan said, and felt that sting at the back of his nose. 'Sort of not. He was on the waiting list for a heart transplant.'

There was silence for a moment. 'Was he the one you were going to go to the football with?' For the first time he heard her sound tentative.

'Penny…'

'Oh, God!' She was a mass of manufactured hormones, not that he knew, and this news came at the end of a very upsetting day. 'He missed the football match because of me.'

'It wasn't something at the top of his bucket list.' Ethan actually found himself smiling as he recalled the conversation he'd had with Phil when he'd told him that he couldn't get the time off, the one about the sympathy vote.

And, no, he didn't fancy Penny, he'd just had a bit too much to drink, he must have, because he was telling her that they'd often gone to watch football. 'He went anyway—with Justin, his son.' And he told Penny about the illness that had ravaged his cousin. 'He got a virus a couple of years ago.' And he could understand a bit better why the patients liked her, because she was very matter-of-fact and didn't gush out her sympathies, just asked pertinent questions and then asked how his son and wife were doing.

'Ex-wife,' Ethan said, and he found himself musing—only he was doing it out loud and to Penny. 'They broke up before he got ill, she had an affair and it was all just a mess. It must be hell for her too and she's coming tomorrow. She's bringing Justin.'

'How old is he?'

'Six,' Ethan said.

She asked how his aunt and uncle were.

'Not great,' he admitted. 'They're worried that they won't get to see Justin so much anymore. It's just a mess all round.'

And he told Penny the hell of watching someone so vital and full of life gradually getting weaker. How he hated that he had only just made it to the hospital in time. He let out more than he had to Kate, to anyone, and during that conversation Penny found out that it had been his sister who had dropped him off at work, but there was no room for relief or dousing of red-hot pokers, or anything really, as she could hear the heartbreak in his voice.

'Thirty-six,' Ethan repeated, and was met by silence. He would never have known that her silence was because of tears. 'So, while I suppose we were expecting it, it still came as a shock.' He didn't really know how better to explain it. 'And it will be a shock for Justin too.'

'Poor kid,' Penny said.

'Anyway, thanks for swapping.'

He hung up the phone, poured his spaghetti on the toast and then frowned because it was cold. He'd surely only been on the phone for a moment and so back into the microwave it went.

They'd actually been talking for a full twenty minutes.

At five a.m. Penny stood, bleary-eyed, under the shower, trying to wake up. She got out and then dried her hair. At least she didn't have to worry about make-up yet, given that she would be crying it all off very soon.

And normally the terribly efficient Penny didn't have to worry about what to wear because her work wardrobe was on a fourteen-day rotation, except it wasn't so simple at the moment because her arms were bruised from all the blood tests and so her sleeveless grey top wasn't an option.

Even the simplest thing seemed complicated this morning.

A sheer neutral jumper worked well with her black skirt, except it meant that she had to change her underwear because it showed her black bra, and with all her appointments and tests the usually meticulous Penny's laundry wasn't up to date. Racing the clock, she grabbed coral silk underwear that she'd never usually consider wearing for work and then raced downstairs, so rushed and tired that by mistake she added orange juice instead of milk to her coffee and had to make her drink all over again.

Still, Penny thought, she was glad to have been able to help out Ethan, and there was just a flutter of something unfamiliar stirring. Penny hadn't fancied anyone for ages. Not since she and Vince had spilt up. Well, that wasn't strictly true—she'd had a slight crush on someone a while ago, but she certainly wasn't about to go there, even in her thoughts. She drove for what felt like ages until at last, at a quarter to seven, she lay with her knees up, loathing it despite being used to it, as she underwent the internal scan to find out how her ovaries were behaving. And if that wasn't bad enough, afterwards she headed for her blood test.

'Morning, Penny!'

They all knew her well.

Penny was determined not to make the scene she had yesterday. She was there willingly after all. But her resolve wavered as she sat on the seat and one of the nurses held her head as she cried while the other strapped down her arm—it was just an exercise in humiliation really.

'I'm not doing this again,' Penny said as she felt the needle go into her already-bruised vein.

But she'd said that the last time, yet here she was again, locked in the exhausting world of IVF.

Penny sorted out her make-up in the hospital car park and was, in fact, in the department well before nine.

'Morning, Penny.' Mr Dean was especially pleased to see her, because it meant that he could soon go home. 'I hope that you had a good night's sleep—the place is wild.'

Of course it was.

'Where's Penny?' was a frequent cry that she heard throughout the day and Penny didn't really stop for a break, just made do with coffee on the run, but by one o'clock she knew that she had to get something to eat, which she would, just as soon as Mrs Hunt's chest pain was sorted out.

'Cardiology knows that you're here,' Penny explained to her patient. 'They haven't forgotten you. They're just a bit busy up on CCU.' The medication patch wasn't working and Penny was just writing Mrs Hunt up for some morphine when the department was alerted that a severe head injury was on its way in.

'Can you sort out that medication, Vanessa?' Penny asked as she pulled on a fresh gown and gloves and her eye shield. 'Maybe you could give Cardiology another page, just remind them that she's here?' Penny said, because one look at her new patient and Penny knew she wouldn't be back in to see Mrs Hunt for a while.

'Fight at school,' a paramedic said as they lifted the young man over. 'Fell backwards...'

The teen was still in his school uniform and was, she was told, eighteen. Penny shut out the horror and focussed on her patient, feeling the mush of his skull beneath her gloved hands.

'CPR was started immediately and continued at the scene...' Penny listened to the paramedics' handover as she worked. He'd been intubated and they'd got his heart started again, but it wasn't looking good at all. She flashed a torch into his eyes but they were fixed and dilated. Still, he'd been given atropine, a medication that, amongst other things, dilated the pupils, which could account for that.

Hopefully.

'Has anyone seen Penny?' She heard Jasmine's voice.

'Curtain one, Resus,' Penny shouted. 'What?'

she asked a moment later when Jasmine popped her head around.

'Nothing.' Jasmine saw the seriousness of the situation and came and helped Lisa with the young man. The trauma team arrived then as well, but despite their best efforts and equipment things were looking seriously grim.

'We'll get him round for a head CT.' The trauma consultant was speaking with Penny and she glanced up as Ethan came in. He was wearing a black suit and had taken off his tie. His face was a touch grey and he looked down at the young man on the resus bed and then at Penny. 'I'm just letting you know that I'm back. I'll get changed.'

'Before you do, could you just check in on curtain three?' Penny said. 'I had to leave her for this.'

Ethan never did get to change. Mrs Hunt's chest pain was increasing.

'Vanessa!' Penny was trying to concentrate on her patient but she could hear a commotion starting across the room. 'Did you give her that morphine?'

'I'm giving it now.'

It was a horrible afternoon.

Once the young patient was being dealt with by Trauma, Penny had an extremely tart word with Vanessa but she was just met with excuses.

'I was trying to get through to Cardiology and then I was waiting for someone to come and check the drug with me, but everyone was in with the trauma or at lunch...'

And Penny said nothing. She didn't have to, her look said it all.

'Two staff members have to check morphine.' Lisa stuck up for her nurse, of course. 'And nurses do have to eat!' Penny bit down on a brittle response, because she'd really love to have made it to lunch too. There was a gnawing of hunger in her stomach but more than that she was annoyed that Mrs Hunt had been in pain for a good fifteen minutes when the medication had been ordered well before that. 'We do our best, Penny,' Lisa said.

It just wasn't good enough for Penny, though she held on to those words.

The police came in and so to did the parents and as the trauma team had taken the young man from CT straight to Theatre, it was Penny who had to speak to them.

'Do you want me to come in with you?' Lisa offered, but Penny shook her head.

'I'll be fine.'

Ethan watched as she walked towards the interview room and thanked God that today it wasn't him about to break terrible news.

'Mr and Mrs Monroe.' Penny introduced herself and sat down. 'I was the doctor on duty when Heath was brought in.'

And she went through everything with them. They didn't need her tears, neither did they need false hope. She told them it was incredibly serious but that their son was in Theatre, and she watched as their lives fell apart. As she walked out of the interview room, Penny wondered if she could really bear to be a mum because the agony on their features, the sobbing that had come from Mrs Monroe was, Penny realised, from a kind of love she didn't yet know.

'How are they?' Ethan asked when she came back to the nurses' station.

'They're just having a nice cup of tea...' Penny bristled and then checked herself. She was aware she was terribly brittle at times. Jasmine had happily told her that on several occasions, but speaking with Heath's parents had been incredibly hard. 'Awful,' she admitted, then looked at his black suit and up into his hazel eyes and she could see they were a little bit bloodshot. Normally Penny didn't ask questions, she liked to keep everything distanced, but she had seen his eyes shutter when he'd looked at the young patient, remembered the raw pain in his voice last night, and for once she crossed the line.

'How was the funeral?' Penny asked.

'It wasn't a funeral apparently, it was a celebration of life.' He turned back to his notes. 'It was a funeral to me.'

'How was the son?'

'Trying to be brave.' He let out a breath.

He looked beautiful in a suit; in fact, Penny couldn't believe that she'd never noticed until recently that he was a very good-looking man. Still, her mind had been in other places in recent weeks, but it was in an unfamiliar one now, because she wanted to say something more to him, wanted to somehow say the right thing. She just didn't know what.

'I need to get something to eat.' Penny, of course, said the wrong thing, but she was actually feeling sick she was so hungry. 'I'm sorry, Ethan, that sounded...'

'It's fine.' For the first time that day Ethan actually smiled. Penny really was socially awkward, Ethan realised. It just didn't offend him so much today.

'Can I have a word, please, Penny?' She turned

at Jasmine's voice, remembered she had been looking for her earlier.

'Away from here.' Penny saw how pale her sister was and even before they had reached her office, Penny couldn't help but ask.

'Is it the baby?'

'No.' Jasmine swallowed before speaking. 'Jed's mum had a stroke this morning.'

'Oh! I'm sorry to hear that. How bad is it?'

'We're not sure yet. Jed's trying to get away from work and then he's going to fly over there.'

'You need to go with him.' Instantly, Penny understood her sister's dilemma—Jed's family were all in Sydney.

'I can't leave you now.' Jasmine's eyes were full of tears.

'Jasmine. Your husband's mum is ill, possibly seriously. How can you not go with him? You know how people had to just drop everything when Mum was sick.'

'You're mid-treatment and I promised you—'

'You made a bigger promise to your husband

when you married him.' Penny was incredibly firm. 'I will be fine.' Jasmine gave her a very disbelieving look. After all, she was the one who gave Penny her injections and knew just how bad she was. 'I will be,' Penny insisted.

'You'll stop the treatment,' Jasmine said.

'I won't. I'll ring the clinic now and make an appointment or I'll go to my GP. Jasmine, you know that you have to go with Jed.'

She did.

There really wasn't a choice.

But what Penny didn't tell her was that there was little chance of her getting to the clinic by six and even if she did, tomorrow she was on midday till nine.

'Are you okay?' Ethan frowned as she joined him at the nurses' station.

'I just had some bad news,' Penny said. 'Jed's mother has had a stroke.'

'I'm sorry to hear that.' He saw tears starting to fill her very blue eyes and her nose starting to go red. 'Are you close?'

'No.' Penny shook her head. 'They live in Sydney, Jasmine is on her way there now.'

'I meant close,' Ethan said, as Penny seemed a little dazed, 'as in are you close to her?'

'Not really. I just met her once at the wedding.' Penny blinked. 'She seemed pretty nice, though. Ethan…' Penny took a deep breath '…could I ask…?' No, she couldn't ask him to cover for her now, because even if he said yes to tonight, what about tomorrow and the next day? 'It doesn't matter.'

She went to walk off to her office and Ethan sat there frowning. Really, all he did was frown any time he spoke to Penny. She really was the most confusing woman he had ever met.

Cold one minute and then incredibly empathetic the next.

Ethan looked up and qualified his thought.

Make that empathetic one minute and a soon-to-be blubbering mess the next. Her face had gone bright red and she had stopped in the corridor by a sink and was pulling paper towels out of the dispenser, and her shoulders were heaving.

He didn't know very much about Penny, she'd made sure of that, but from the little that he did know, Ethan was quite sure she would hate any of the staff seeing her like that. She was trying to dash off, but Lisa was calling out to her and he watched as the trauma registrar came into the department and caught a glimpse of her and, patient notes in hand, went to waylay her. Ethan stepped in.

'I need a quick word with you, please, Penny.' He took her by the elbow and sped her through the department into one of the patient interview rooms, and the second they were inside Penny broke down.

CHAPTER SIX

'PLEASE, GO, ETHAN.'

He just stood there.

'Ethan, please, just go.'

'I'm really sorry about your sister's mother-in-law.' He saw her forehead crinkle and then intermingled with sobs she let out a strange gurgle of laughter.

'It's not that.'

'Oh.'

'I'm not that nice.'

Ethan stood there awkwardly, not knowing what to do. He could handle tears from patients and their relatives but this felt more personal than that. She had a handful of paper towels so he couldn't even offer her a tissue.

Then she blurted it out.

'I'm having IVF.'

And any fledgling thoughts that possibly he might rather like Penny in *that* way were instantly doused. Still, at least, in this, he did know what to do. My God, he did, because he wrapped his arms around her and gave her a cuddle. As he did so he was filled with a sense of déjà vu, because his twin sister had been through it so many times and had taught him what to do. Often Kate had wept on him, on anyone who happened to be passing really.

Except there was no feeling of déjà vu when he actually held Penny in his arms. She was incredibly slim and, he was quite sure from her little wriggle to escape, that she wasn't someone who particularly liked to be held. 'It must be horrible,' Ethan said, because Kate had told him that that was a good thing to say when he'd messed up a few times and said the completely wrong thing.

'I'm a mess,' Penny mumbled.

'You're not a mess,' Ethan said. 'It's just that

your hormones are crazy at the moment.' He would ring Kate tonight and thank her, Ethan thought as he felt Penny relax in his arms. Then he ventured off the given script. 'So that's what's been going on?'

She nodded into his chest and Ethan realised then that her on IVF was the only Penny he had ever known. 'It's my second go. That's why I was away when you started here. I should have taken time off this time.'

He realised now why she'd been so inflexible with the roster on other occasions, all the appointments she would have been juggling would have made it impossible to change—and yet yesterday, at short notice, she had. 'Why didn't you just say?'

'I didn't want anyone to know. But now I'm just being a bitch to everyone.'

'You're not.'

'Everyone's saying it.'

'No,' Ethan lied, 'you just come across as a bit tough.' He gave in then. 'I bet you're normally a really nice person.' He held his breath, worried that he had said the wrong thing, but he felt her laugh a little. 'I bet you're a sweet, warm, lovely thing really.'

'No,' Penny said. 'I *am* a bitch, but you've just met the exacerbated version.' And then she started to cry again. 'You missed going to the football with your cousin because of me. I'm a horribly selfish person.'

'Penny, stop it.'

Except she couldn't stop crying, just wished she could take back that day and he could have had that time with his cousin.

'Phil and I often went to football, it really wasn't a big deal, and remember Phil got to spend precious time with Justin that day.'

Finally she felt herself calming, embarrassed now at being held, and she pulled away.

'You need to go home,' Ethan said. 'Were you at the clinic this morning?'

Penny nodded.

'I can cover more for you now that I know.

You come in to work a bit later some mornings, just text me.'

'It's not just because I'm tired that I'm crying.' She took a big breath and told him the embarrassing truth. 'I'm terrified of needles and Jasmine has been the one giving the injections to me. I'm due for one at six. I'm going to ring the clinic and see if they can give it to me, but I'm not sure what time they close, and then there's tomorrow...'

Ethan sat her down. 'Surely one of the nurses can give it to you?' Ethan suggested, but realised that, of course, she didn't want anyone to know she was on IVF. 'I can give you your injections.'

'God, no.' Penny shook her head. 'I'm not just a little bit scared of needles. I get in a right state sometimes—even worse than I am now.'

'Can't your partner come in?' Ethan asked, because Carl had given Kate hers. 'Surely he'd—'

'I don't have a partner. I'm doing this by myself.'

'You're doing this on your own?'

'Yes.'

'You mean you'd choose...' As Penny looked at him sharply, luckily Ethan had the good sense to stop talking. He just couldn't really believe someone would choose to be a parent, let alone a single one—babies really weren't his forte. But, whatever his thoughts on the subject were, they really weren't relevant here. Penny wasn't asking for his opinion, just some help with logistics. Instead, he asked where the clinic was and then looked at his watch.

'You really do need to get going if you're going to have a hope of making it there, but if the travelling gets too much, any time you need me to give you an injection, I'm more than happy to.'

'I don't think you realise how bad I am with needles.'

'There's a straitjacket in the lock-up room,' Ethan said. And he wasn't joking, there *was* a straitjacket in the lock-up room and he knew exactly how petrified some people were of needles. 'I do know how to give an injection to someone who doesn't want one, Penny. I tend to do it quite a lot.' He gave her a smile but she shook her head.

'I'll sort something out.'

'Go, then,' Ethan said. 'And thank you for today.'

Of course, it wasn't quite so straightforward as simply leaving the department and getting to her car. Three people stopped Penny on her way to her office, which she had to go to, because that's where her bag and keys were, and also her medication.

Penny dashed to her car and pulled out of the car park, ringing the IVF nurse as she did so and being put straight on hold.

Penny hit the beach road and it wasn't five in the morning, it was nearly five p.m., so the traffic was bumper to bumper. Ringing off, she turned the car round—it took fifteen minutes just to get back to work.

'I thought you'd be back.' Ethan smiled.

'Can I talk to you for a second?' She just had

to let him know what he was getting into. 'I need these every night at six. I don't know how long Jasmine is going to be gone and we don't always work the same shifts.'

'I know I'm lousy at commitment, Penny,' Ethan said. 'But I think I can manage this. I can come into work if I'm not on, or you can come into me, or we can meet in a bar and go into a quiet corner.' He almost made her smile.

'From the noises I make they'd think you were attacking me!' Penny said. 'I'm not just a little bit scared of needles—I try not to, but sometimes I start crying. I just lose it.'

'It's fine.' He was annoyingly calm.

'I don't think you understand. You will not calm me down and even if I say no, I don't want it, you have to ignore me. Just undo my skirt and stick it in.'

'I'm not even going to try to respond to that.' Ethan saw the flush spread on her cheeks and he met her eyes with a smile. 'Go and get something to eat and sit down for a while and then remind me closer to six.'

Penny tapped him on the shoulder at five to six.

'Could I have a word in my office, please, Ethan?'

'Of course.'

'I need you for a moment, Penny,' Lisa called as they walked past.

'It will have to keep.' Ethan's voice was gruff. 'Only buzz me if something urgent comes in. I need to speak with Penny.'

'It sounds as if I'm about to be told off.'

'Exactly,' Ethan said. 'So we shan't be disturbed.'

They walked into her office where Penny had things all set up and, she noted, he actually thought to lock the door. 'Is this what you were doing when I knocked for you to come for a drink with Gordon?'

Penny nodded.

'You really never know what goes on behind

closed doors.' He gave her a smile and then, ever the doctor, he checked the vials and the use-by dates.

'I've already checked everything.'

'Good for you,' Ethan said, refusing to be rushed and taking the time to make sure, but it was all too much for Penny. It was bad enough that she was having a needle, but with Jasmine gone and everything it was just a whole lot worse. Seeing Ethan pick up the syringe, Penny started to cry, and not as she had before. This was, Ethan realised, the sound of real fear.

'Okay.' He kept his voice practical, he was just going to go in and get this over and done with.

'No!' Penny shouted. She had worked herself up to try and stay calm. She could think of nothing worse then Ethan seeing her in such a terrible state and having to face him again, but her resolve had completely broken when she'd seen him pick up the injection. The last thing on Penny's mind was the result and the possibility of a baby; she just wanted to get out of there.

'No.' She said it again as he walked over with the kidney dish. 'Ethan, no, I've changed my mind.'

'Tough.'

Even as Penny said no, she was trying to undo her skirt and failing, and then when Ethan stepped in she tried to brush off his hands but failed at that too.

'Ethan, please!' Penny was doing her best not to sob and make a complete fool of herself. He put the kidney dish down on the desk behind her, his hands finding the side zip of her skirt. He pushed her against the desk and held her in place with one hip as he pulled her skirt down a little bit and reached for the alcohol swab on the desk behind him. Then Ethan turned her, resisting and crying, around and she felt the coldness of the alcohol on the top of her buttock. 'What the hell are you doing?' Penny shouted. 'It's sub-cut, you idiot…'

He turned her quickly to face him and before

she even knew it, Ethan had swabbed her stomach and the needle was in.

'I know.' Ethan smiled, massaging the injection site with one hand as he threw the needle into the kidney dish with the other. 'That's called a distraction technique, in case you were wondering.'

Only the distraction had been for him—the image of coral-coloured silk knickers and just a glimpse of the top of her bottom were branded in his mind. Now he was looking down at her lovely pale stomach as he massaged the injection in, and he saw the dots of bruises and his fingers wanted to wander there too. More than that he knew she was watching his fingers, knew he should stop now, or that she could take over, but they both just stood very close, looking down. And he actually wondered if it was wrong just how turned on he was now and, no, he did not want to fancy her.

It had been a hell of a day, a completely wretched day, and he blamed it on the funeral as he lingered a little too long. And Penny looked at his mouth and blamed it all on the hormones she was taking, because she was holding back from kissing him.

'Okay!' It was Ethan who took control, whose mind sort of jolted and alerted him to the fact that the woman he was very close to kissing, the woman he was hard for now, was very actively trying to get pregnant.

'You're done,' Ethan said. He picked up the kidney dish, turned his back and made a big deal about tipping the contents into the sharps dispenser.

She was a close colleague too, Ethan told himself. And an absolute cow to work with, he reminded himself a few times—except he knew why now.

No, he did not want to fancy Penny.

As Penny did up her zipper and smoothed down her blouse she was not sure what, if anything, had happened just then. She was embarrassed at her tears, of course, but there was something else swirling in the room with them, an energy that must not be acknowledged.

'Thank you.'

'No problem,' Ethan clipped. 'Same time tomorrow, then?'

'Please,' Penny said. 'I mean, yes.'

CHAPTER SEVEN

ETHAN WAS ACTUALLY on a day off the next day.

He woke late, saw the black suit over the chair and tried not to think about yesterday.

Tried not to, because it had been a day of hellish emotion and it seemed impossible to think that Justin would be back at school today and the world was moving on, but not for some.

The transplant co-ordinator had been called up for the head injury patient, Heath, later in the evening, he had heard. Ethan had seen the boy's parents sobbing outside the ambulance bay on his way home.

Waking up to grief was a lot like waking up with a hangover, Ethan decided as he pieced together the previous day and braced himself to face the upcoming one. He lay there, eyes closed, trying to summon up the energy to move, to get on with his day. He should maybe ring his aunt and uncle, Ethan thought, see how they were, but he couldn't stomach it. Or ring his sister and find out how the rest of the wake had been.

Except he just wanted to be alone, just as he had wanted to be alone last night. He hadn't been able to face a bar. Even Kelly, a friend, who was more than a friend sometimes, had called, and knowing how tough the day would have been had suggested coming over.

He hadn't wanted that either.

He could go and do something, maybe a long drive down to the Ocean Road, just stay a night in Torquay or Lorne perhaps, watch the waves, get away, except, just as he thought he had a plan Ethan remembered he had to be at the hospital at six to give Penny her injection.

Penny.

Ethan blew out a breath as he recalled the near miss last night.

What the hell had he been thinking? Or rather, he hadn't been thinking in the least.

Still, he kept getting glimpses of coral underwear flashing before his eyes throughout the day.

He'd expected flesh coloured.

Not that he'd thought about it.

But *had* he thought about it, then flesh coloured it would be.

Sensible, seamless, Ethan decided as he drove to the hospital. Not that she'd need a bra.

Not that he'd noticed.

Ethan pulled into his parking spot and tried to go back, tried to rewind the clock to a few days ago, when he hadn't remotely thought of her in that way. When she had just been a sour-faced colleague who was difficult to work with, one who hadn't turned round and bewitched him with a smile.

'What are you doing here?' Rex asked as Ethan walked through the department, for once out of scrubs and dressed in black jeans and a black top.

'I need to take some work home. Is it just you on?' Ethan asked casually.

'Nope,' Rex said. 'Penny's on.' He pulled a poker face. 'She's just taking a break.'

Ethan knew that because he'd texted her to say that he was here, but he didn't want anyone getting even a hint so he stood and chatted with Rex a moment before heading to Penny's office.

'Sorry to mess up your day off.'

He checked the dose again, and she undid her zipper and just stared at the door as she lowered her skirt. Penny closed her eyes and hyperventilated but managed to stay much calmer, even if her knuckles were white as she clutched the desk behind her. In turn, Ethan was very gruff and businesslike and what they had both been silently nervous about happening was nowhere near repeated. In fact, it was all over and done with very quickly.

'Thanks for this.'

'No problem,' Ethan said.

'Will you carry on working?' Ethan asked, and Penny frowned as she tucked her shirt in. 'When you have the baby I mean.'

'If I have one,' Penny said. 'Did you ask Gordon the same question?'

'No.' He was so not into political correctness. 'But then again, Gordon isn't a single dad. And,' he added, 'despite his account of it, Gordon wasn't actually the one who got pregnant and gave birth.'

Penny laughed.

'Shall we go and see them?' Ethan said. 'It's quiet out there at the moment and Rex is in. We could head up and just get it over with.'

'Get it over with?' Penny smiled. She had been thinking exactly the same thing. Gordon really could be the most crushing bore and she'd never really had a conversation with Hilary, a paediatrician, that hadn't revolved around baby poo.

'Sorry.' Ethan didn't know he was being teased. 'That was a bit...'

'Don't you like babies?' Penny asked as they headed towards the lifts that would take them to the maternity unit.

'Actually, no.' Ethan was honest. 'I don't actively dislike them or anything. My sister has had three now. I like the five-year-old, he makes me laugh sometimes.'

'How old is your sister?'

'Thirty-six,' Ethan said, and she remembered their phone conversation.

'You're a twin.' Penny smiled. 'On anyone else that would be cute.'

They stopped at the gift shop and bought flowers and balloons and Penny wrote a card but Ethan had forgotten to get one and asked if he could just add his name.

'You're giving me injections,' Penny said. 'Not sperm. Buy your own card.'

She was the most horrible person he had ever met, but she did make him grin, and Ethan was still smiling when they both walked into Hilary's room together.

'Penny!' Gordon seemed delighted to see them. 'Ethan!' He shook Ethan's hand. 'He's just woken up, we're just feeding.'

'Well, don't let us interrupt you. We just came in to give you these and say a quick hello.'

'Don't be daft,' Gordon said. 'Completely natural. What do you think? He's a good-looking little man, isn't he?'

Ethan peered down at the baby and to Penny's delight he was blushing. 'Congratulations,' he said to Hilary. 'He's very handsome.'

'He's gorgeous,' Penny said. 'He looks like you.'

'He looks like Gordon,' Hilary corrected her.

She could feel Ethan's exquisite discomfort beside her and to his credit he did attempt conversation, but she almost felt him fold in relief as his phone bleeped and he excused himself for a moment.

'I heard about Jed's mum,' Hilary said. 'Have you heard any news?'

'She's actually improving,' Penny said as

Ethan came back in. 'They should be home in a couple of days.'

'I'm hoping to get him home soon.' Hilary looked down at her baby. 'He's a bit small, though, and the labour—'

Thankfully Penny's pager crackled into life, urgently summoning her down to Emergency.

'I'll come and see if they need me too,' Ethan offered.

'That was you.' Penny grinned as they fled out of Maternity.

'I'm sorry!' Ethan said. 'I just couldn't sit there while she fed the baby. I'm fine with patients, with women in cafés, but when I know someone…' He was honest. 'I was the same with my sister. I just break out in a sweat. Please,' he said. 'I beg of you, when you have your baby, please don't feed it when I come to visit.'

'I promise I won't,' Penny assured him.

'I know that sounds terrible.'

'Absolutely not.' Penny could think of nothing

worse than feeding a baby in front of Ethan. 'I don't even know if I want to feed it myself.'

'Stop!' Ethan said. He just didn't want to think about Penny and breasts and babies and the black panties she was wearing today.

Yes, he'd seen, even if he'd tried very hard not to.

'Sorry.' Even Penny couldn't believe she was discussing breastfeeding with him. 'You don't approve, do you?'

'Of bottle-feeding?'

She didn't smile at his joke. 'I meant you don't approve of me doing this on my own.'

'I can't really say the right thing here.'

'You can,' she offered, because she didn't mind people's *invited* opinions.

'No.' He was honest. 'I just can't imagine that someone would choose to be a single mum. My mum raised my sister and I on her own and it wasn't easy.'

'My mum got divorced,' Penny said, 'and, believe me, things got a whole lot better when Dad wasn't around.' Then she checked herself. 'Actually, things got a whole lot worse for a couple of years, but then they got better. And my sister was a single mum for a while.'

'By choice?'

'No,' Penny said. 'Well, yes, by choice, because she had no choice but to leave Simon's dad. I really have thought things through.'

'Tell me?'

'I've got to work.'

'Dinner?' Ethan said, because he really was starting to like Penny, well, not fancy like, he told himself, but then he remembered the flash of her knickers and what had almost happened yesterday. Maybe he should recant that invitation to take her out for dinner, except he'd already asked.

'Why?'

Ethan shrugged. 'Well, I've been out with a new father and listened to his labour and if I add a woman going through IVF, I figure by the end of the week I could qualify as a sensitive new-age guy.'

Penny smiled and he had been right—she really was attractive when she did.

'Okay, then.' Her acceptance caught him just a little by surprise. He'd sort of been hoping, for safety's sake, that she might decline. 'Tomorrow,' she said. 'After you stab me.'

Penny was on a day off, so it was she who '*dropped in*' just as Ethan was finishing up.

She was wearing a dress that buttoned up at the front and her heels were a little higher. He caught the musky scent of her perfume as he followed her into the office and locked the door.

'I'll do it,' he said, taking her little cool bag.

She told him her doses and he heard the shake in her voice as she did so.

'I am so sorry about this.' He turned and she was trying to undo the little buttons on her dress. It really was a very genuine fear, made worse today because she'd had the whole drive here to think about it. Ethan actually saw her break out into a cold sweat as he approached and she was trying very hard not to cry.

'I need a bit more skin than that, Penny.' She'd only managed two buttons. 'Here.' He undid a couple more and felt the splash of a hot tear on the back of his hand. 'You must really want this baby.'

'I do.'

He could see tiny goose bumps rising on her stomach. He was really impressed with himself because he was completely matter-of-fact and, despite a glimpse of purple underwear and the heady scent of her, he was not a bit turned on. Two evenings in a row now!

He just kept reminding himself that there'd be a baby in there any time soon and that those small breasts would soon look like Hilary's.

'Done,' Ethan said.

'Thanks.'

'Where do you want to go and eat?'

Penny didn't care, so they ended up in the same

pub near the hospital where he had been with Gordon, and they took a booth and sat opposite each other. He saw the dark smudges under her eyes and the paleness of her skin. The treatment must really be taking its toll by now.

'Jasmine's coming back the day after tomorrow,' Penny said. 'Well, as long as Jed's mother keeps improving, so tomorrow should be the last time you have to do it.'

'It's not an issue.'

'I am very grateful to you, though. Jasmine was worried that I'd just stop the treatment and I think she was right.'

'Have you told her I'm giving them?'

'Yes.' Penny nodded. 'She sends you her sympathies.'

He'd prefer self-restraint.

'When's your next blood test?'

'Seven a.m. tomorrow.'

'Do you want to change the next one?' Ethan asked. 'Go in a little bit later?'

Penny shook her head. 'Thanks, but it has to be done early.'

She ordered nachos smothered in sour cream and guacamole and cheese, and it surprised him because he'd thought she'd order a salad or something.

And usually she would but this was like PMS times a thousand so she just scooped up the cheesiest bit she could find and sank her teeth into it with such pleasure that Ethan wished he hadn't ordered the steak.

'Have some.' She saw his eyes linger on them.

'Who'd have thought?' Ethan said.

'I'm good at sharing.'

'I meant the two of us being out together. What a difference a week can make.'

Penny smiled and he rather wished she hadn't.

'How come you're so petrified of needles?'

'I'm not as bad as I used to be,' Penny said. 'I did hypnosis, counselling and everything, just to get to where I could let someone give me one.'

'So you think hypnosis works?'

She saw his sceptical frown. 'I don't know,' Penny admitted. 'I mean, I'm still scared of needles but the hypnotherapist did get me to remember the first time that I freaked out—I was at school and we were all lined up to get an injection and the girl in front of me passed out.'

'Mass hysteria?'

'Possibly.' Penny had thought about it practically. 'But my father had just left my mother a couple of weeks before, so apparently, according to the counsellor, it was my excuse to scream and cry.' She gave a very wicked smile. 'Load of rubbish really.' She took a sip of her drink. 'All I know is that the fear is there and I'm having to face it over and over and over. Sometimes it's terrible, sometimes it's not so bad. I was good at my blood test this morning.'

'You were good tonight.'

'Yep,' Penny said. 'And had Jasmine's mother-in-law not had a stroke, you'd never have known and we'd have been able to look each other in the eye.'

'I'm looking you in the eye now, Penny.'

She looked up and so he was. She saw that his eyes were more amber than hazel and there was a quickening to her pulse. How could she possibly be thinking such thoughts? She couldn't be attracted to Ethan. She had to stay focussed on her treatment—her plan to become a mother. Except thinking about babies had her thinking about making babies the old-fashioned way! With Ethan?

It was very warm in the bar; it must have been that causing this sear of heat between them, and Ethan wished he'd asked for his steak rare because it was taking for ever to come.

'Do you have any phobias?' she asked when thankfully his order had been delivered and normality was starting to return.

'I don't think so.'

'Flying?'

'Love it.' Ethan smiled.

'Heights?'

'They don't bother me in the least.'

She did, though, Ethan thought as he ate his steak and tried to tell himself he was out with a colleague, but Penny was starting to bother him a lot, only not in the way she once had. He was just in no position to say. To his absolute surprise where Penny was concerned, since that morning when she'd turned round and smiled, there had been a charge in the air.

One that to Ethan really didn't make sense, because he liked his women soft, curvy and cute, which was a terrible word and one he'd never admit to out loud, but that was what he liked.

And there was nothing soft about Penny and there wasn't a curve to be seen, and as for cute...

'What are you smiling at?' Penny frowned.

'Nothing.' He reminded himself of the reason they were actually out. 'So,' he asked, 'assuming this round of treatment is a success, how many embryos are you having put back?' He saw her blink at the rather personal question.

'Two.'

'I think I've just found my phobia.'

Penny grinned. He made no secret of the fact he had no desire to ever be a parent, so she asked him why.

'I'm not sure really,' Ethan admitted. 'It's the responsibility, I guess. I save it all for work. I've just never wanted to settle down, let alone have a baby.' He gave her a wide-eyed look. 'And certainly not two at the same time.'

'Twins would be lovely,' she said, 'then I'd never have to go through this again.'

'You should speak to my mum first,' Ethan said. 'I guarantee if you did you'd only put one back.'

'You said she was a single mum?'

'No,' he corrected her. 'I said that she raised us on her own. My father died when we were six.'

'I'm sorry.' She looked at him. 'Same age as Justin.'

He gave a small mirthless smile, her hit just a little too direct.

'How did you deal with it?'

Ethan gave a shrug. 'You just grow up overnight.' He never really talked about it with anyone. 'It's tough, though. I heard Vera, my aunt, telling Justin to be brave, and it was all the same stuff she told me. Then there was Jack, my uncle, he's my dad's brother, giving me lectures over the years about how I was the man of the house and I needed to be more responsible. I hope they don't say the same to Justin, it scared the life out of me.'

Maybe that was why he held on to his freedom so much, Penny mused, and she couldn't help asking more.

'And were you the man of the house?' Penny asked, and she gave a thin smile when he shrugged.

'I tried to be,' Ethan said. 'And resented every minute of it. Then being a teenager sort of got in the way of being sensible.'

'Did you miss having a dad?'

They were both being honest, and after all she had asked, and he wasn't going to sugar coat his response just because it was what she wanted to hear.

'Yes,' Ethan said. 'But I do accept that things are very different now. Back then there weren't so many women raising children alone. I used to feel the odd one out. I'm sure that yours won't feel like that.' He reminded himself to smile. 'Anyway, what would I know?'

They ordered coffee and then chatted about work, about her case review tomorrow, where once a week the senior staff got together and reviewed a case. It was Penny's turn and, no, she told him, she wasn't nervous. 'Just ill prepared,' Penny admitted. 'So I'd better get home and rectify that.'

They walked out to their cars and there was a strange moment because had she not been doing her level best to get pregnant, had they just been out, Ethan would have done his usual thing and kissed her. Right now that would prove no problem at all, because as they stood by her car, he actually forgot about needles and ultrasounds and little people that made an awful lot of noise and demanded to be fed a lot.

''Night, then,' she said, going into her bag for her keys and then looking up at him.

''Night, Penny.'

He went to give her a kiss on the cheek, but changed his mind midway. Except it was too late for that so he went ahead, but there was an awkward moment because he missed his mark and his lips landed a little close to her mouth.

He felt the warmth of her blush on his lips and knew he should say good night and walk away. Except he wasn't holding a needle and she wasn't crying or asking him to stop and he could smell her hair and that musky perfume. He thought of the purple underwear he had glimpsed earlier.

It was all just a second, a very long second, and Penny was a guilty party in this too. Had been complicit as she'd carefully selected her underwear that morning, was as attracted as he was and, yes, she wanted his mouth. Now here it was, just the graze of his lips, and she felt as if a feather was stroking her from the inside. There was just a flare that lit between them and mouths that were a beat away from applying pressure, but neither did. Just two mouths mingling and deciding to linger, two minds racing and about to quiet and give in, but then they were literally saved by the bell, or rather by his pager.

'Did you arrange that one too?' Penny asked.

Ethan just grinned, because had he been thinking straight he might have arranged one for a few moments ago because he did not want to start anything with Penny.

Well, not Penny.

He didn't want to start anything with a soon-to-be-pregnant Penny, Ethan reminded himself as he telephoned work to find out what was happening.

'The place is steaming,' Ethan said when he came off the phone.

'Should I come in?'

'It's packed and they're not getting through

them. I'll just go in for a couple of hours and help them clear the backlog. You go home.'

'You're sure?'

Ethan nodded, gave her a light kiss on the cheek that was definitely just a friendly one, a token effort to erase the one that had happened before, saw her into her car and then headed to his.

One more needle to get through, Ethan told himself.

He was almost as nervous about it as she was.

CHAPTER EIGHT

PENNY KNEW THE drill only too well.

After a very sleepless night, trying to prepare for her case presentation then later going over and over their near kiss, Penny was up at the crack of dawn and about to have her ultrasound. She went to hitch up her skirt, but she was wearing her wraparound dress and it was a bit too tight.

'Just open it up, Penny,' the sonographer said, and offered her a sheet, which she pulled over not just her stomach but her chest, because everything was exposed.

Damn.

She had been dressing for her presentation.

Or had she?

Penny honestly wasn't sure.

It *was* her presentation outfit, which had been sitting in its dry-cleaner bag for two weeks now, waiting for today. It was her grey wraparound and even though she didn't have a cleavage, it was a bit too low so underneath she wore a silver-grey cami with a bit of lace at the top, and because it was Penny she wore matching panties, which were rather more lace than silk.

And tonight she'd be getting her needle from Ethan. It was too much, Penny decided. She'd just change into scrubs, except there was a part of her that wanted his eyes on her, a part of her that refused to be silenced, that wanted more than last night, and Penny was most unused to such strong feelings. Even now, walking to get her blood done, she was thinking of the near miss last night and what might have unfolded if they hadn't been interrupted by the pager. She blinked in astonishment at the depravity of her own thoughts.

'Morning, Penny.'

It took two attempts to get the blood this

morning. She was stressed about her case presentation, worried about her choice of clothes,
exhausted after a night of thinking and trying
not to think about Ethan and a kiss that never
happened and must never happen! This meant
Penny sobbed like she never had as they took
her blood.

'Finished.' The nurse smiled as she pressed
down on the cotton swab. 'I think I left a bruise.'

'It's my own fault,' Penny said, because despite being held down her arm had jerked when
the needle had gone in. As Penny blew her nose,
instead of standing up and getting out of there
as quickly as possible as she usually would, she
asked a question. She was a typical doctor and
had read up on things herself, but there was one
bit now that was honestly confusing her. 'Can I
ask a question?'

'Of course.'

'About…' She was going bright red but tried to
sound matter-of-fact as she spoke. 'Increased libido?' Her voice came out as a croak and Penny

cleared her throat, but the nurse was completely unfazed by her question.

'You're a walking cocktail of hormones at the moment, Penny,' the nurse said. 'Often women could think of nothing worse at this stage, but for some…'

'So it's normal?'

'Sure. Just make sure that you use protection,' the nurse said. 'It's only once we've done the embryo transfer that you need to refrain, and not just from sex, no orgasms either—which is unfortunate…' she smiled '…because an increase in libido is commonplace then.'

Penny blinked. She'd sort of skipped over all those parts, thinking that it would never really be a problem for her.

'You'll get a phone call later and we'll sort out your doses,' the nurse said. 'You'll be ready for your trigger injection any day soon. So just enjoy it for now.'

She certainly wouldn't be enjoying it! Penny just wanted these feelings to pass, wanted a neat explanation as to why she was nearly climbing the walls at the thought of Ethan. Did she fancy him or was it the medication?

And did it really matter?

Would it be so terrible to have sex with someone you really fancied even if it was going absolutely nowhere?

Stop it, she told herself as she drove to work.

Just stop it right there!

Of course the second she walked into work she saw Ethan. She tried to douse the fire in her cheeks, only it wasn't working—he was dressed in scrubs and very unshaven. He was scowling at the bed board and had clearly been up all night.

'Good sleep?' His voice was wry.

'Fantastic.' Hers was equally wry as she walked past, because she'd be lucky to have slept for more than a couple of hours, though she was glad now that she hadn't accepted the consultant's position. There was no way she could have juggled it all, she would not have coped if she'd been called in last night and had still been expected to work through the next day.

Penny got through the busy morning, doing her best to avoid him, and she had a feeling Ethan was trying to avoid her too. Both were trying to pretend that the near miss last night hadn't happened.

She headed to the lecture theatre and set up her computer, nodding a greeting as her colleagues filed in. She wasn't nervous as she was a very good public speaker, but her heart was fluttering as Ethan walked in. He'd been firing on coffee all morning but from his yawn as he took a seat in the lecture theatre for her presentation, she wouldn't be in the least surprised if he fell asleep midway through.

Penny had decided not to present about Heath, the young man with the head injury, and instead spoke about the renal patient who had come in with cardiac failure. She went through it all— the medication, the dosages, admitted to her own hesitation—suggesting a protocol sheet be implemented, and Ethan didn't fall asleep as she spoke. Instead, he watched her.

Watched her mouth move and speak, but hardly heard a word, his mind more on her pert bottom as she turned and pointed to the white-board. All he wanted to do was go home—why did he have to fancy Penny?

He knew that the extra jewellery and make-up and heels were not for his benefit. It was the way Penny was and she was always going to make an extra effort for this type of thing. Except he could see the flash of lace on her cami and he wanted the effort to have been for him.

Then his eyes lingered on the tie of her dress and his mind wandered as to how he was going to get it off, or up, and it was then that she caught him looking. Her voice trailed off and they both just stared.

Really stared.

Ethan clamped his teeth together because he was incredibly tempted to silently mouth something *really* inappropriate to her, just to see those burning cheeks flame further.

'Penny?' Mr Dean asked when the silence dragged on. 'You said he was then given a bolus?'

'That's right.' She snapped back to her presentation and apart from that, apart from nearly jumping off the stage and straddling Ethan, Penny got through the rest of her speech really well. Attempting to be normal, Ethan congratulated her a little while later.

'Well done,' he said. 'I'm sorry if I offended you that day. I didn't mean to just walk in and take over.'

'But you didn't offend me.' Penny frowned and then remembered. 'I was having a hot flash, Ethan.' She watched his face break into a smile. 'It was the drugs—that was a glimpse of menopausal Penny.'

'Well, remind me, if we're both still working here then, that it's time for me to look for another job,' Ethan said laughingly.

'Are you heading off, Ethan?' Mr Dean walked past. 'You were here all night.'

'Soon,' Ethan said, then he looked at Penny. 'If I go home now I'm going to crash and I won't get back.'

'I'm so sorry.' He really did look exhausted.

'I'm going to go into the on-call room and sleep,' Ethan said. 'Get everything ready and then come and get me at five to six.'

'Thanks.'

She tried to ignore the on-call room, but every time she walked past, the thought of Ethan lying in there asleep flashed like a strobe light in her mind. If she was like this now, what the hell was she going to be like after the embryo transfer? She might be needing that straitjacket after all.

Penny set up her needle and swab and had it all laid out in her office and then, because she could at times be nice, she made Ethan a coffee before she knocked on the door of the on-call room. He was so zonked she could actually hear the low sounds of snoring.

'Ethan.' She knocked again and put her head around the door. 'Ethan, it's nearly six.' He sat up and sort of shook himself awake.

'Can you bring it in here?' He just wanted to get the injection over and done with and then go back to sleep but then he changed his mind and with good reason. 'I'll be out in a minute.'

'I brought you a coffee.'

She walked over in the darkness and he got a waft of her scent. He heard the slight rattle as she put his coffee down on the bedside table and it was right that her hand was shaking, Ethan thought, because she was seconds away from being pulled into his bed.

'Thanks,' Ethan said. 'I'll be there soon.'

He had to get himself under control—physically and mentally—before touching her.

Hurry home, Jasmine.

He'd never met Jed, let alone his mother, but he wished her the speediest, most uneventful of recoveries from her stroke. Ethan gulped his coffee and splashed his face in the sink and then walked to Penny's office.

'Ready?'

'Yes.' She was fiddling with the tie of her dress and he could hear her starting to cry, just sort of breathy sobs that she was trying to keep in.

'Okay, then.' He walked towards her, and she was a mess, a hot mess at that, Ethan thought as he looked at her eyes. They showed a mixture of fear and lust and if she said no to the injection this time, he would drop the needle.

He didn't want her to do this.

He wanted her to stop so that they could do what people who fancied each other did.

A lot.

He wanted to go out and have more dinners and have nachos himself next time and go far too far in a car park and then go even further back home.

'No.' She pushed at his hand as it reached for her dress tie, and he was breathing very hard now—tired, turned on, pissed off. He didn't want to do this either.

'What do you want, Penny?' He forgot he wasn't supposed to ask, he was supposed to go ahead and give her the needle. Her hands were on his arm and he tried to ignore the feel of her fingers on his skin. He tried to undo the tie for her as if he hadn't been thinking about doing just that all day.

She had on silver-grey knickers and a matching cami, and through the silk he could tell her chest was almost completely flat. He liked curves, Ethan told himself, except he wanted his mouth to lower to the thick nipples he could see rising out of the fabric, and as he swabbed her stomach he caught a glimpse of blonde hair above her panty line and he could see a bit through the lace too.

And he did *not* want to give her this needle. He could hear her gulping and soft whimpers and feel her breath on his cheek, and he did not want to do it.

But he'd signed up for the gig so he swabbed her skin and though he hesitated over her stomach, he finally stuck the needle in.

'There,' he said. 'You're done.'

Ethan rubbed her stomach and then she took over. His hand did not linger, he just wanted this over and done, wanted out and home. Maybe tonight he'd call Kelly, get this Penny fantasy out of his head once and for all.

Then he saw the lust in her eyes and her lips were moving towards his and he jerked his head backwards. 'Penny!' he warned.

She screwed her eyes closed at his rejection. She'd have to resign, it was all just so unlike her. 'I'm so sorry, Ethan. I think it's the drugs, it's like I'm on heat.'

He'd embarrassed her, Ethan knew that, which he'd never wanted to do. She had no need to be embarrassed. He wanted her too, so he tried to soften things, except he was rock hard. 'I just don't want to start something with someone who's trying for a baby.'

'I know. I get that completely. I'm never like this…' She attempted her excuses again as he dropped the needle into the dish behind her. 'It's the drugs.'

'It's not the drugs, Penny,' Ethan said, because he wasn't taking any, but hormones were certainly raging and he stopped fighting it then, his mouth coming down on hers the way it had wanted to last night.

She almost came just at the pressure of his mouth as her stomach hollowed with lust. It wasn't a brief kiss, it wasn't unsure and whatever the opposite of tentative was should be called Ethan, because his tongue was deliciously crude, his unshaven jaw surely shredding her skin. Penny was no saint either. Her hands were in his hair, her scantily clad body pressing into him, feeling his fierce erection, and he pulled away just a little.

'Penny…'

'I know,' she said. 'I know this is going nowhere.'

'You understand?'

'Of course.' She was in her office, with her dress undone, and it was all so inappropriate, especially for someone like Penny, so much so that she fought an incredible urge to laugh. Then she stopped fighting and laughed a little bit. 'If you knew me, you'd know that it *is* the drugs. I'm going to be so embarrassed later.'

'Why?' He smiled down. 'It's just a kiss,' Ethan said, 'a one-off.'

'An anomaly,' Penny said. 'Never to be repeated or mentioned again. As soon as you walk out the door we're done.'

'I'm not out the door yet.'

She was more than happy with the ground rules, just for the bliss of the return of his mouth.

It was just a kiss but it was a kiss with a secret. His fingers were working her nipples through the silk of her cami till she moaned in his mouth and then he slipped his hand up the cami so that skin could meet skin. He worked them a little more firmly. Normally she loathed that, hated the beat of disappointment when they found out that she really was quite flat-chested, but it just didn't matter right now. If anything he was even more turned on because he pressed his erection hard into her, and she almost came undone—a ball of hot tension in his arms.

And it was still just a kiss, but the secret was deepening, his hand now sliding into her panties, and they would both never repeat or mention it again, but in this too he knew what to do. He cupped her for a moment before he began to stroke her with precision, and he couldn't for a moment kiss and concentrate, so he let her mouth work his neck, and then he warned her to be careful because there must be no evidence, and as she removed her mouth, Penny lost her head.

She just gave in to the bliss and the scent of him, her hands around his neck to steady herself, her legs shaking as she fought the urge for him to lift her, to wrap her legs around his waist, yet she stood as she forgot how to breathe.

Ethan felt the rip of tension and her quiver and her thighs clasp around his hand and he stroked through her pulses as frantic need left her and leached into him, and he got back to kissing her, but with urgency. Pressing himself hard into her, Ethan's hands moved to lift her, a fierce need to be inside her, but then sense reared its head and moved into his and he released her hips, because if he didn't, he would have her over that desk.

And, no, Ethan told himself, that he did not want.

Except he did.

No wonder he didn't like being responsible, Ethan thought, peeling them apart. 'And now I'm handing you back to Jasmine.' He looked down and smiled and she looked up and nodded, and there was that awkward bit, because she had come and he hadn't, and she wanted more too, yet he was releasing her, about to head out there to where this had never happened.

'Ethan…' She wanted more of him, wanted more than a corner of chocolate before it was wrapped and returned to the fridge, and she didn't care if they were in her office; right now, she simply didn't care.

'Penny.' He gave her a small kiss to interrupt her invitation, and then he made it very clear where they were. 'You go and concentrate on getting that baby.'

CHAPTER NINE

IT WAS ALL happening.

It was like a train she had boarded and she so badly wanted the baby at the end, but she'd lost something along the way. Ethan was a bit aloof and she was back to being frosty but she missed the Ethan she had glimpsed and, in turn, he wanted more of Penny, just not *that* much more.

Because Ethan knew what was happening now. He didn't turn a hair when she asked if they could swap their days off at short notice.

'Sure,' was all he said.

He asked no questions, though he did look things up on the internet, knew that when she came back after her couple of days off, there was a high chance she would be as horny as hell.

But no orgasms allowed, Ethan thought with a black smile as he knocked on her office door to update her on one of her patients.

'I feel like a delivery boy,' he said, holding a card and chocolates.

She wished she had a delivery boy who looked like Ethan—she'd be ringing for pizza every night, Penny thought as he handed his wares over. 'Heath's parents asked me to give these to you.'

'You should have buzzed me.' Immediately Penny stood, but Ethan shook his head.

'I went to, but they were getting upset so they asked if I could just hand these to you. I think they were a bit overwhelmed being back in Emergency.'

Penny nodded and sat back down.

'I spoke to them for a bit,' Ethan told her.

'How were they?' Penny asked as she read the letter.

'Just struggling through. They said they knew that one day they'd be pleased with the decision they had made for Heath to be a donor, but not yet.' And Penny nodded because the letter said much the same—thanking her for her care that day and for gently preparing them for what was to come a few hours later. She showed the letter to Ethan and as he read it he forgot to be aloof, forgot he didn't really want to be talking with Penny at the moment.

'I couldn't have dealt with it that day,' he admitted.

'I'm not surprised.'

'Phil used to feel guilty about that. He said he was lying there basically hoping someone would die.'

'You can't think like that.'

'But you *do* think like that,' Ethan admitted. 'Because even I was thinking that if Phil had lasted for just a few more days...'

'There are a lot of people waiting for hearts.' Penny said, practical with the facts. 'And a lot of hearts are wasted. How's Justin dealing with it all?'

'I don't know,' Ethan admitted, and saw the rise of her eyebrows. 'It's all a bit of a mess. Gina wants nothing to do with Phil's side of the family and I can't say I blame her. She wasn't exactly treated well by my uncle and aunt.' He gave a tired shrug. 'Anyway, there's nothing I can do.' He went to ask how she was doing, but changed his mind—he really didn't want a conversation about egg retrieval and a five-day wait before embryo transfer. 'I'd better get back out there.'

'Sure,' Penny said, but there was an impossible tension between them.

And so they muddled through and it was a bit easier to be aloof than he'd thought it might be, because he was a bit fed up too, not just with Penny but with himself. He didn't particularly like the superficial Ethan who, a couple of weeks later, had this guilty image of Penny's test results being negative and asking her for a night out in the city to cheer her up and then taking her back to his apartment to make love, not babies.

And, yes, he was glad it was a long weekend

coming up and that in one hour from now he'd be out of there.

Hopefully without seeing Penny, because she was about to start a stint of nights and was off today.

Then, just when he thought he'd got through it, in Penny walked. She had Jasmine's toddler son with her—must be picking him up from crèche to help Jasmine out. He saw Jasmine give her a brief, excited hug, saw Penny warn her to hush, and even without that, Ethan knew that she was pregnant, he just knew from the timing, because he'd been back on the IVF site again.

And, no, there was no avoiding her and no avoiding the fact he was crazy about a woman who was pregnant, and not with his child.

'Hi, there.' Jasmine had taken Simon to the vending machine and he came over when she caught his eye. 'Ready for nights?' he asked.

'As I'll ever be.'

'So?' he asked, because even if he didn't want to know, he knew. 'How are you?'

'Good,' Penny said, and her back teeth clamped down because she wanted to tell him her news but it was far too early. But more than that she wanted to flirt, she wanted him and he was just out of bounds. She wanted dates and dinners and laughter and fun, yet she badly wanted the baby inside her too. 'What are you doing for the long weekend? Anything nice?'

'Yep.' Ethan nodded. It had been a long day and now, with the unspoken news hanging between them, more than ever he just wanted to get away. 'I've got the long weekend and then two days off, I'm not back here till Thursday. I'm going out on a boat and hopefully we'll all be eating too much, drinking too much and talking too much.'

'With friends?' She thought her face would crack from smiling.

'Family,' Ethan said. 'We do it every year.'

'Sounds great,' Penny said. 'Kate will have her hands full.' Penny could imagine nothing worse than being at sea with toddlers—she'd have a nervous breakdown.

'God, no.' Ethan pulled a face. 'Once a year my mum has them all for her so she can get away. Kate says it keeps her sane. It would never happen otherwise.'

'I don't blame her,' Penny said. 'She'd be worried sick trying to keep tabs on them on a boat.'

'I meant I wouldn't be going if she brought them.' He hesitated, tried to turn it into a joke and then stopped, but he'd said it all, really—he was Mr R&R, heading off, kicking back and just so removed from the world she was about to join.

'It sounds lovely,' Penny said, because a few nights out at sea with Ethan, well, there was not a lot she could think of that sounded nicer than that.

He looked at her for a very long time, wished she could come along, could almost see her in a sarong with sunburnt shoulders, and he couldn't help but regret all the things they could have done, all the dates they could have been on and he was, for a ridiculous moment, tempted to ask her to see if she could swap her nights with someone and come with him, but he stopped himself, because even if the impossible could be achieved, he soon saw the real picture.

No wine, because she wasn't drinking.

No seafood either.

And throwing up on the hour every hour as Kate had done one year.

'Have a good break,' Penny said.

Oh, he fully intended to!

Only it wasn't that great.

Given what had had happened in recent weeks, it was a far more sombre affair, of course.

'You're quiet,' Kate commented on the Saturday morning. It was a glorious day, the sky blue, the wind crisp and the sun hot.

'I think we're all quiet,' Ethan said.

'I rang Gina.' Ethan looked over, hoping there had been some progress, but Kate shook her head. 'I said maybe we could get the kids together, but she said no. Surely she can't keep Justin from his grandparents?'

'I guess she can,' Ethan said. 'Or she can make it as difficult as possible for them to see him, which she is.' He shook his head. 'I'm staying out of it.'

'Ethan, you can't do nothing.'

'I can,' he interrupted, 'because if I say what I really think about the situation, it's going to be a few very long days at sea.'

'Say it to me,' Kate pushed.

'Are you sure?' He looked at his sister, who nodded. 'Phil should have sorted this.' He watched her jaw tighten and Kate struggled for a moment before she could respond.

'He didn't know this was going to happen.'

'Yes, he did,' Ethan interrupted. 'I told him to sort this. I told him he had to work things out between his parents and Gina. Phil knew full well the mess he'd be leaving behind if he didn't sort something out. I know he did, because I told him. Frankly, I don't blame Gina for wanting to have nothing to do with us. Maybe Jack and Vera should have thought about the future before they opened their mouths when Gina had the audacity to break up with their son.'

'No one knew then how sick Phil was going to get.'

'No one ever knows what the future holds.' Ethan refused to turn Phil into a saint and even if his aunt and uncle were grieving, it didn't suddenly make them infallible. 'I love Jack and Vera and I loved Phil, but the fact is that some of this mess is of their own making,' Ethan said. 'See now why I'm staying out of it?'

Kate nodded and looked at her rarely angry brother and was positive something else was eating him. 'Is there anything else going on?'

They were close, they were twins and they spoke a lot, but Ethan had only once before said what he was about to. 'I like someone.'

Kate saw his grim face. 'Married?' she groaned.

'No.'

'How long have you known her?'

'Since I started my new job, well, just after. She was having a couple of weeks off.'

'What's she like?'

'Moody, angry, funny, single...'

'Kids?' Kate checked, because there had to be a 'but'.

'Pregnant.' He looked at his sister. 'Only just.'

'Ethan!' Kate couldn't keep the excitement from her voice, but she didn't get carried away when she saw his face. 'I know you said it's not for you, but—'

'The baby's not mine!' Ethan quickly interrupted. 'Penny's on IVF. She's determined to be a single mum, she'd already started her treatment when we met.'

'Oh, Ethan.'

'I was giving her the shots.'

'Why?'

'Because she's petrified of needles and I didn't fancy her then, or maybe I did.' He shook his head. 'Kate, I don't even think I want kids, you know it broke Caitlin and I up. But even if I could somehow wrap my head around that, I mean even if I'd met Penny and she already had a child...' He pulled a face. 'I don't know, Kate. I can't walk around watching her get bigger with someone else's child.'

'Ethan,' Kate said. 'You know Carl and I were both having problems.' She was very careful not to say too much, but he knew that they had both been having problems, that all three of their children were Carl's in everything but genes.

'I get that,' Ethan said. 'But I bet Carl took a bit of time to get his head around it, and I bet he said a few things while he did that he wished he could take back now.'

And Kate stayed silent, because her brother was right—it had taken a lot of talking and a lot of soul searching before Carl had come round. 'And that was with two people who both desperately wanted kids and I don't even know that I do. I just walked in on the end of Penny's decision and I'm supposed to be fine with it? Well, I'm not and I'll tell you this much. I can't even...'

He shut his mouth. He wasn't going to discuss *everything* with his sister and he couldn't explain properly, even to himself, the strange possessiveness that had gripped him when he'd almost slept with Penny.

'What do *you* want, Ethan?'

'Penny,' Ethan said. 'But I want time with Penny. I want to get to know her some more, it's still early days. I don't want to start something with someone who has a baby on board and be the one holding the sick back when I didn't cause it.' He looked at his sister. 'Selfish?'

'Honest.'

'And I'm angry too.'

'Why?'

'It doesn't matter.'

'Ethan?'

'It really doesn't matter,' Ethan said, even though he hated it when others did that. 'Because it's not relevant now.'

They couldn't carry on talking as they were being called for. The engines were still and he stood there as Phil's ashes were scattered. He looked at his aunt and uncle, who had been so strong at the funeral, celebrating his life, weep as the wind carried away the last thing they could do for him.

Only it wasn't just Phil that Ethan was thinking about as they stood in silence on deck. He wanted Penny to be happy, he was pleased for her, just terribly disappointed for them. Maybe he could do it, maybe he would wrap his head around it in a few months' time, but he felt as if there were a gun to it now and he looked at the ashes sinking into the waves and he was crying.

Not a lot and he didn't stand out, there wasn't a dry eye on board. He had every reason to be choked up, but he was, Kate knew, shedding a tear for other reasons too.

Penny didn't mind working nights, and she was actually glad that Ethan was on leave because she just wanted a pause to sort out how she felt about him. She wanted the hormones to calm down so she could look at things a bit more objectively. Not that she'd had even a moment to think about Ethan tonight; the place had been busy from the start of her shift and she was trying to put an NG tube down a very restless patient.

'Come on, Mia, swallow,' Penny said. 'You need this.'

'I don't want the tube.'

'Then you have to drink the charcoal.'

Mia had taken an overdose and to stop the tablets from being absorbed further, she had to be given a large drink of activated charcoal. It looked terrible, it was black and chalky, but as Penny and Vanessa had told the patient over and over, it actually didn't taste too bad. It was all to no avail, though—despite a lot of coaxing they'd only managed to get half the liquid into Mia.

'If you can let me put this tube down your nose and into your stomach, we can put the rest of it down and you won't have to taste it,' Penny said, 'and then you can have a rest, but it's imperative that you have the charcoal.'

'I can't.' The poor girl was upset already—after a huge row at her boyfriend Rory's house she'd stupidly swallowed some pills and when she'd got home her parents had thought she'd been drinking. When Mia had finally admitted what she had done, before calling the ambulance, there had been another row for Mia with her parents shouting at her, even as the paramedics arrived.

They'd started shouting again when Rory had arrived at the hospital, when most of all Mia needed calm, and Penny was doing her best to ensure that Mia got it, but first she *had* to get the charcoal in.

'Do you want Rory to come in?' Penny suggested. 'He offered before.'

Mia nodded and Penny called the young man in. At eighteen Rory was very mature and he held both Mia's hands as Penny got ready to have another go at putting the tube down.

'Big breath,' Penny said, 'and then start to swallow when the tube hits the back of your throat.'

Except she didn't swallow. Instead, Mia vomited all over Penny's gown, so much so that it soaked through to her clothing.

'It doesn't matter,' Penny said soothingly as Mia started sobbing her apology. 'Let's give it another go.'

The cubicle looked as if someone had been playing with a black paintball and the staff and patients didn't look much better either, but finally the tube was in. Penny checked its position, relieved that the tube was in the right spot.

'Right, let's get the charcoal in and then you can have a rest.' The medication was poured down and Penny had a word with the intern, Raj, before she headed to the changing rooms. She was incredibly tired and couldn't wait for the couple of hours till the end of her shift.

Penny kept a spare set of clothes at work, but it was five a.m. and she was past caring so, rarely for her, she pulled some scrubs off the trolley, filled the sink with water to try and soak her shirt, and it was as she did so that Penny felt it—a cold feeling down below. She wanted to be imagining things, wanted to be wrong, so she dashed to the loo, but as she pulled down her panties it was confirmed that, no, she wasn't imagining things.

'Please, no,' Penny begged as she sat with her head in her hands, trying to tell herself it was normal, just some spotting, that it wasn't her period she was getting.

Penny couldn't stand to call it a baby; it was the only way she had been able to get through it last time. So she told herself that it was just a period, said over and over to herself that most women wouldn't have even have known that they were pregnant at this stage.

Except Penny knew that she fleetingly had been.

'Penny!' She heard Vanessa come into the changing room.

'Can I have two minutes?'

'Mia's not well.'

'I'm on my way,' Penny said through gritted teeth.

'She's seizing,' Vanessa went on.

'Then what are you doing in here, talking to me?' Penny shouted. 'Put out an urgent page for the medics.'

As Vanessa fled, with shaking hands Penny had to find change to buy a pad and then pulled on scrubs and dashed back to Mia. Raj was there and had given Mia diazepam; she had stopped seizing but was clearly very unwell.

'She's taken something else,' Penny said, because the medications Mia had admitted to taking would not have caused this.

'I've just spoken to the family.' Vanessa's voice was shaky. 'The boyfriend's ringing his mum to go through all the bins and things as they were at his house when she took them.'

'Good.'

Penny was tough, she *had* to be tough, she just

didn't let herself think about personal things; instead she focussed on saving a sixteen-year-old girl who had made a stupid mistake that might now cost her her life. As soon as Rory came off the phone she spoke to the distressed boyfriend to try and get more clues as to what Mia might have taken.

'Mum's on anti-depressants.' Rory looked bewildered. 'I didn't even know that she was, but she's had a look and one of the packets is missing. She thinks—'

'Okay, what are they called?'

He told her and Penny kept her expression from reacting—she didn't want to scare the young man any more than he already was, but tricyclic antidepressants were very serious in overdose and could cause not just seizures but cardiac arrhythmias.

Leaving Rory, Penny told the medics what the young girl had taken and then dealt with the parents, who were still blaming the boyfriend.

'He has been very helpful,' Penny said. 'If it

wasn't for Rory, we wouldn't have known what Mia had taken, and he also helped us to get the tube down. Mia's actually had the right treatment—the charcoal will stop any further absorption, but she'll need to go to Intensive Care for observation.'

'When can we see her?' the father asked.

'I can take you in there now,' Penny offered, because Mia was awake now, though very drowsy, but first she just wanted to clarify something with the parents. 'I know you're very upset at the moment, but it has to be put aside for now. Mia needs calm, she is not to be distressed.' Penny looked up as Rory walked in.

'What the hell did you say to upset her enough to take all those pills?' the father flared. 'You caused this.'

'I'm sorry!' Penny stood. She'd heard enough. 'Until you calm down, you're not coming in to see Mia.'

'You can't stop me from seeing her.'

'Absolutely I can.' Penny stood firm. 'Mia is

to be kept as calm as possible. We're trying to prevent further arrhythmias or seizures, not actively bring them on.'

She walked off and started writing up her notes, and finally a rather more contrite father asked if he could go in and see his daughter now, assuring Penny he would not cause her any further distress.

'Of course.'

She stepped behind the curtain to have a quick word with Vanessa before letting them in.

'Mia's parents want to come in,' Penny said. 'Don't take any nonsense from the dad if he starts getting angry. Just ask him to leave.'

'I don't take nonsense from the patients and their relatives,' Vanessa said, and as Penny turned to go she heard the nurse mutter, 'I've got no choice with the staff, though...'

Penny didn't have the time, let alone the emotional capacity, to respond to Vanessa, or even to dwell on it. She had no alternative other than to drag herself through the last part of her shift, then she got into her car and finally she was home.

Penny took off her scrubs. Her stomach was black from the charcoal and she showered quickly then put on a nightdress and picked up the phone.

'I'm bleeding.'

The IVF nurse was very practical and calm and, yes, a bit of spotting was normal, but this was more than a bit of spotting and they went through the medications, but Penny could feel herself cramping.

'Should I rest?' She wanted to ring in sick but she knew deep down that it wouldn't make any real difference.

But she rang in sick anyway.

Work was less than impressed, because it was the long weekend and one consultant was out on a boat and Mr Dean was on a golf weekend, but whether or not it would make a difference to the outcome, Penny couldn't have gone into work anyway—she just lay in bed, trying to hold on to something she was sure she'd already lost.

'I'm sorry, Penny.' It was Tuesday night. She'd actually stopped bleeding but didn't dare hope, yet there was a tiny flicker there when she took the call, only to hear that her HCG levels were tumbling down.

All that for twenty-four hours of being pregnant.

Jasmine's periods were later than that sometimes.

'Oh, Penny, I'm so sorry!' Jasmine, who the second she'd heard that Penny had called in sick, had been in and out of her home all over the weekend. She was there too when the nurse called with her blood results and Jasmine wrapped her in a hug when Penny put down the phone after the news. But Penny could feel Jasmine's belly soft and round and pressing into her stupid empty flat one and Penny said some horrible things.

Horrible things.

Like, no, actually, Jasmine didn't understand.

And that it was all right for Jasmine to stand there and be so compassionate and understanding when she didn't actually have a clue how it felt to not even be able to get pregnant. Except it was a bit worse than that because Penny used the F word and then asked her sister to get out.

'Penny, please!'

'No!'

She was back to being a bitch.

CHAPTER TEN

THERE WERE DISADVANTAGES to being a consultant, as Ethan was finding out, because when he came back from his long-awaited days off, which had actually turned into more of an extended wake, half his colleagues were sulking because he'd been out of range and they'd been called in to work.

'Penny's sick?' Ethan frowned when Lisa told him.

That Penny might be ill wasn't the problem apparently, though it was the problem for Ethan. 'We had a locum for two nights and Mr Dean came in, but he wasn't too pleased.' Lisa brought him up to speed.

'But if she's sick, she can't help it,' Ethan pointed out as a knot tightened in his stomach. 'When did she ring in?'

'Saturday morning.' Lisa sighed. 'At the beginning of a long weekend. It's been a bit grim here, to say the least.'

But it wasn't just Penny they were annoyed at.

'Did you have a good break?' Mr Dean gave a tight, mirthless smile as he walked past, but Ethan just rolled his eyes. He didn't give a damn about things like that—he worked hard when he was here and was entitled to his days off. The only person Ethan was worried about now was Penny.

Except when he tried to call her, she didn't pick up her phone.

'How's Penny?' Ethan asked a worried-looking Jasmine when she arrived for her late shift.

Jasmine's cheeks flushed and she just gave a brief shake of her head.

'Did she lose it?'

Ethan grimaced when Jasmine gave a reluctant nod.

Ethan headed to his office and rang Kate and told her the little he knew.

'Don't call it *it*,' Kate suggested.

'I didn't mean it like that.'

'I know,' Kate said. 'Poor thing.'

'I don't know what to do.' Ethan didn't even know how he felt. He was gutted for Penny as he thought of all she had been through.

But there was guilt there as well.

'I don't know what you can do either,' Kate admitted, because Carl had been as invested in the procedures as she had and had been right there beside her when on many occasions the news hadn't been good. But though she utterly understood where her brother was coming from, he wasn't going to react as Carl had.

'Do I just not mention it? I mean…'

'No,' Kate said, but then halted. 'I don't know. You said she hadn't told you she was pregnant?'

'I can't just ignore it,' Ethan said. 'She won't pick up the phone.'

'You really like her?'

'Yes.'

'Then I think you ought to go over there and just be ready.'

'For what?'

'For anything.'

Even as he rang the bell, Ethan had absolutely no idea if he was doing the right thing.

It just couldn't go past without being noted.

That was all he knew.

She opened the door in her dressing gown, except it was undone and underneath she had on a short nightdress. Ethan hadn't known many woman who wore silky nightdresses and matching dressing gowns, but this was Penny, he reminded himself, and even if she was a bit washed out, she still looked stunning.

'I'm so sorry, Penny.'

She looked at him, all brown and healthy and brimming with energy from nearly a week off, and she felt drab and pale in comparison. 'How do you know?' Penny asked. 'Did Jasmine say something?'

Ethan hadn't even made it through the door and he'd already put his foot in it. 'No,' Ethan said. 'I asked her when I heard you'd called in sick.'

'She shouldn't have said anything.'

'She didn't say a word,' Ethan said. 'I asked if you'd…' He breathed out. 'Penny, I knew before you went away that you were pregnant.'

'How?'

How? Because she was buried so deep in his skull, he'd been on IVF sites and working out dates and watching her unseen, constantly tuned in to her, though she didn't need to hear that. 'I just knew,' Ethan said. 'Jasmine didn't say a word.'

Penny opened the door further and let him in.

'I didn't know what to bring.' He was very honest with his discomfort and it helped that he didn't try to hide it. It helped that he had come too.

'Wine would have been nice.'

'I can go out and get some.'

'I've got some open.' Penny looked at him warily. 'I'm not very good company.'

'I'm not here for a party.'

'Well, you won't get one. I'm boring even me now in my quest for a baby, so I'd run for the beach now if I were you. I know it's not your thing. I'll be back to normal soon.'

'Come here,' he said, and he gave her a cuddle. She wriggled a bit as she had the first day he'd held her and then she gave in; it felt really nice to be held by him.

'Do you want me to go out and get a bottle?'

'No. I'm drinking alone. Well, not alone, I've got my cat.'

And an ugly cat it was too, Ethan thought as feline eyes narrowed in suspicion at a big male stomping through the room. He followed Penny to where she was retrieving her glass and bottle from her bedside table and hovered at the door.

'I'm a cliché,' Penny said. 'I'll be the mad aunt, if Jasmine ever lets me see them again.' She closed her eyes. 'I had a terrible argument with her when I found out. I'm a horrible sister.'

'I'm sure you're not.'

'I am.' Penny sniffed. 'We've never been that close, but for the last few months we've both really tried, and now I've gone and ruined it. I told her that she had no idea how I felt.'

'She doesn't,' Ethan said.

'But she tries so hard to. It's not her fault, I just…' She was embarrassed to admit just how bad she'd been, but was too guilt ridden to gloss over it. 'She gave me a cuddle and I could feel her stomach and I told her that, no, she didn't know, but I said it more nastily than that.' Worried blue eyes lifted to him and a dark blush spread on her cheeks. 'It wasn't just that she's pregnant, though.' She stopped. She certainly wasn't about to share her shameful truth. 'It doesn't matter.'

'Tell me.'

'I can't.'

'You can.'

'I really can't.'

'I hate that,' Ethan said. 'I hate it when people go, oh, it doesn't matter, when clearly it does, and then they say they can't tell you, and you know that it's something relevant, except you're not allowed to know.'

She actually smiled a little when she responded to him. 'You're *not* allowed.'

'Fine.' Ethan sulked.

'If I told you and you ever said anything, I'd have to kill you.'

Ethan couldn't help but smile but more than that they were sitting down on the sofa together and Penny was, Ethan realised, actually going to reveal. 'When my mum was bought in in cardiac arrest, it was awful. I mean, just awful. Jasmine was on duty but I managed to keep it from her...'

'While you worked on your mum?'

'And I was upset. I mean, really upset.'

'I would imagine so.'

'And Jed gave me a cuddle, nothing more.

What I didn't know then was that Jasmine was seeing Jed. Confused?'

'Not yet.'

'But Jasmine saw us together, before she knew about Mum, I mean…'

'And thought you two were together?' Ethan checked, and Penny nodded. 'And were you?'

'Never.'

'Not a little bit?' Ethan checked.

'Not a smudge,' Penny confirmed. 'But…' She just couldn't bring herself to say it.

'You liked him?'

'A bit.' She was just this ball of guilt. 'I wasn't having dirty dreams or anything.' She went red as she looked at Ethan, because she was having the rudest ones about him. 'But, yes, I sort of liked him. I don't remotely in that way now, I mean that, but at the time…'

'It hurt to find out they were together.'

'Yes,' Penny admitted.

'And now she's got the baby.'

'Two.'

'Penny.' Ethan was honest too. 'Can I tell you something?' He took her hands. 'I think it's completely normal to like someone, to fancy them. I like and fancy people all the time, it's not an issue, even if the two of you…'

'Nothing happened.'

'Which makes things a whole lot easier. But…' he didn't really see the issue '…suppose,' Ethan said, 'just suppose Jasmine was single, and given all we've done is had one kiss, well, a bit more than that…'

And Penny felt the heat of breath in her nostrils, and it burnt a whole lot more than it had with Jed, except she couldn't really tell him that when he was trying to prove a point about how inconsequential it was.

'Okay, bad example.' Ethan scrambled for other scenarios. 'Suppose—'

'I get your point.' She did. In one fell swoop he'd made her realise just how teeny her feelings for her—unknown at the time—future brother-in-law had been. She thought of Jasmine walking alongside her on the beach, admitting how gorgeous Ethan was, and what a tiny deal it had been then.

'You've done nothing wrong,' Ethan said. 'Are you not supposed to like anyone, just in case your sister might?'

'I guess.' Penny couldn't believe how easily a simple conversation had dispersed the complicated into nothing. 'I don't want Jed, and I am pleased she's pregnant.' She looked at Ethan. 'It was just all too much that day. Do you ever feel jealous that Kate has a family?'

'No.' He was honest. 'I just can't imagine ever being settled like that, just one person for the rest of your life. And…' he gave a shrug '…I think we've found another phobia of mine.' He took a deep breath; there was one thing he needed to know. 'Will you try again?'

'I don't know,' Penny said. 'Probably. But they like you to wait a couple of months.'

'You're thirty-four, Penny,' Ethan said.

'Thirty-five,' Penny said. 'It's my birthday.'

He didn't know what to say.

And clearly neither did Jasmine, because the phone rang then and Penny took it into her bedroom. It was a very short, terse phone call and when it was over Penny looked up at him in the doorway, only this time he came in.

'Do you ever fight with your sister?' she asked as he sat with her on the bed and put his arm around her.

'Not really,' Ethan said.

'With anyone?'

'No.' He gave her a smile. 'You.'

But it wasn't enough for Penny. She wanted him to have done something as terrible as she had, and so he thought for a moment, searched his brain for someone he'd had a huge stand-up row with, just to make her feel better.

'With Phil.'

'When?' Penny frowned.

'Last year. There was stuff that needed dealing with and Phil wasn't dealing with it. And I told him so and pretty loudly too.' Ethan gave her a nudge. 'So if you feel bad, imagine having a shouting match with someone who has a heart like a balloon about to burst.'

'But it didn't.'

'No, it didn't. Well, not for another year.' Ethan shook his head; he wasn't going to go there.

'You really loved him, didn't you?'

'Yep.' Ethan nodded. 'But I'm here about you.'

They were lying on the bed now, more two friends chatting than this being about anything sexual, even as the conversation turned to sex. 'Have you ever thought about going about it the old-fashioned way?' Ethan asked. 'Meet someone, fall in love, live the fairy-tale.'

'Been there, done that. Well, I thought it was love and we were frantically trying for a baby for a very long time.'

He'd been doing really well, Kate would have been proud of him, but he grimaced a bit then and she noticed.

'What?'

'Nothing.' Ethan shrugged. He just didn't like

the image of her *frantically* trying with someone else.

'I'm not very fertile—I'm sub-fertile. Isn't that the most horrible word? It put a terrible strain on our relationship. It wasn't just that, though, he was…' She was about to say it didn't matter, but Ethan hated it when she did that. 'Vince was all for the modern working woman, or so he said, yet I was the one who was going to be the stay-home mum.' Ethan looked at her. 'I earned more than him, yet it was just assumed that I'd be the one to stop work.' She saw him frown. 'What?' Penny asked again.

'Why, if you're doing all you can to have a baby, would you want to work?'

'I love my work, I'd go crazy without it, but I would certainly slow things down. It wasn't just that, though, there were other things.'

'Like what?'

'Like I was starting to resent that it was always me stopping at the supermarket on the way home from work and getting dinner. Aside from the fact that I can't have babies, I don't think I'd make a very good wife.'

'What's for dinner, Penny?'

He made her smile.

'What about you?'

'I have no idea,' he said, and turned and smiled at her now-frowning face on the pillow beside him. 'I've never had my fertility checked.'

'You think you're funny, don't you?'

'I know I am,' Ethan said, 'because you're trying really hard not to smile.'

'I meant, have you been in a serious relationship?'

'Apparently,' Ethan said. 'Though I didn't know it at the time.' He sighed at the memory. 'I thought it was great, she wanted to move in...'

'Oh.'

'Or look for somewhere to live, or get engaged and then married and make lots of babies one day.'

'What was her name?'

'Caitlin. I led her on apparently, but I didn't

know that I was, I just thought we were having a good time. I didn't realise it had to be leading somewhere—so now I make things a little more clear from the start.' He waited, his eyes checking that he had.

'I get it, Ethan.' She gave him a smile and then she told him. 'Jasmine said I should have a wild fling with you before I got pregnant.'

'I'm that much of a sure thing, am I?'

'Apparently,' Penny said. 'She thought I should forget about making babies and just enjoy myself for once.'

'Have you ever had sex for the sake of it?' He screwed up his face. 'I mean, how long since you've had sex without trying for a baby?'

'A very long time.' She looked at him. 'There was one time that I would have, but he declined.'

'Well, maybe he was just being all male and territorial and couldn't quite get his head around...' He screwed up his face again, tried to spare the details. 'You know in a few days' time you...'

'Might have been pregnant?'

'No, not just that.'

Penny frowned and then got it. 'With someone else's baby!' She actually laughed. 'You *are* a caveman!'

'Nope, just a normal man.' Ethan grinned, glad to see her smile. 'And the only one I want you *frantically* describing is me.'

And he was getting his words wrong, because he meant that he didn't want to sit here and listen about her ex and her in bed, or did he mean that he wanted to give her something to frantically describe?

That wasn't what he'd come here for.

'I'm going to go.'

He pulled up on his elbow and gave her a kiss, though it was a bit pointless to pretend it was a friendly one, given what they'd been like, and that they were lying on the bed, but Ethan did kiss her with no intention other than to say goodbye.

Except he'd forgotten just how much he liked

kissing her till he was back there, and Penny
was remembering all over again too. It was so
nice to be lying down being kissed by him, nicer
too when a little while later his hands crept to
her breasts that clearly didn't disappoint because
she could feel him harden against her thigh as
he stroked.

Only this time he did what he had wanted to
that time, his mouth moving down, slipping
down the fabric and licking around the areola
and then taking her in his mouth.

She was on her back, his expert mouth suck-
ling her hard, and Penny was gasping, wanting
to turn to get to him, to explore him too, but
loath to end the bliss of his mouth.

He turned her to him, gave her other breast the
same attention. Ethan, who loved breasts, actually loved that she hardly had any. Penny was
grappling to pull out his top, desperate to feel
his skin as his mouth sucking her breast drove
her to higher pleasures.

But Ethan moved her hands away, his intention to take his time, but as his hand slid down the jut of her hips, her nightdress had ridden up and he found his hand cupping her bare bottom. 'Hell, Penny,' he moaned, 'have you been walking around all this time with no knickers on?' He blew out a breath, remembered then the reason he was there, and when Kate had said to be ready for anything, he was quite sure she hadn't meant that. 'Sorry.'

'For what?'

'Taking things too far.'

'You've never taken things too far,' Penny said. 'You haven't taken things far enough.'

They were at each other again, a knot of arms and legs and deep kisses, her hands going to his buckle, but he halted her.

'Penny.' He took her face in his hands and he wrestled with indecision, not sure if it was Hot Mess Penny he was talking to, whom he completely adored and could deal with, or Baby Making Mode Penny, who terrified him, and she got that much.

'I'm not asking you to get me pregnant.'

'Isn't it too soon?' Ethan checked.

'Nope.' And she thought of sex for the sake of it, and how lovely he had been and how badly she wanted the rest of that chocolate bar out of the fridge now. And so too did Ethan. They were back to kissing, only pausing to strip the other off and pray for condoms in his wallet, which, hurrah, there were.

She buried her head in his chest and smelt and felt close-up and naked Ethan. He was stunning, muscled but not too much with a smooth tanned chest and flat brown nipples that shifted from view as his mouth slid down again, only this time not to her breasts. He licked down to her stomach and he did what he had wanted to do that first day he had given her her injection, and he kissed her till she was writhing.

Penny had felt like a pincushion these past weeks, a failed baby-making machine at times, but his mouth was slowly turning her back into a woman as he lingered at each step. Penny closed her eyes in bliss as his mouth moved lower still and with each measured stroke she lost a little more control but gained mounting pleasure. Her hands pulled tight on his hair as Ethan revelled in the taste of her. The scent that had been alluring him for weeks was now his to savour and he carried on kissing her deeply there as she throbbed to his mouth and he returned her to herself.

A new self.

'Ethan.' Penny lay catching her breath, went to say something, she didn't know what. She wanted to sit up and face him, wanted to go down on him. It took a moment to realise it wasn't her decision to make. He was over her, sheathed and poised at her entrance.

'Love-thirty,' he said, sexy and smiling and not a moment too soon for Penny, through with being patient.

She moaned as he filled her. Ethan folded his arms behind her head so that her face was right up to him, and she had forgotten how lovely sex could be. Or rather, Penny amended as he moved deep inside her, she'd never really known just how lovely sex could be. Then, as Ethan shifted tempo she made one final amendment before she lost rational thought. She'd never known sex could be so hot.

She didn't get poor-Penny sex; she got the full bull in Ethan. A surprise birthday present that had her as wild as him. One of his arms moved down to her hips and he practically lifted her off the bed each time he thrust into her. Had Penny ever had any doubt as to all those times she'd thought him aroused, they were gone, because every missed opportunity, every subdued thought Ethan had had seemed to be being banished now over and over deep in her centre.

His want, his desire, the absence of tentativeness had Penny flooded in warmth, her legs wrapping around him, her skin scalding, grinding into him as she tipped into climax.

'Penny…' Ethan was trying to hold on, but feeling her shatter, feeling her jolt as if she'd been stunned, by the time he felt her strong, rapid clenches Ethan was on the way to meeting them.

Almost dizzy, he collapsed on top of her and then moved to the side, pulling her with him, more than a bit bewildered about what had happened, because Ethan loved sex but had never had sex like that, and while going down on her his intention had been to be gentle.

'Did we land on the beach?' Ethan asked.

'I'm not sure,' Penny admitted. 'I can't actually see.' She felt a gurgle of laughter swirl inside her, only it wasn't laughter, she realised, just this glimpse of being free. 'And it's actually thirty-fifteen now,' Penny said. 'You forfeited the last game if I remember rightly.'

He'd had no idea what to expect when he'd arrived tonight at her door, but felt as if, in that small conversation, he'd met the real Penny, the one that he'd sometimes glimpsed. Or was it more that it was a different him? Usually Ethan was snoring his head off right about now, but instead it was Penny dozing as he went and dimmed the lights before climbing into bed beside her.

'Happy birthday, Penny.'

And as she lay there, feeling his big body beside her, she thought that it really shouldn't have been a happy birthday; it had had every ingredient for it not to be, except it had just turned into her most memorable, possibly favourite one.

'Thank you,' Penny said, and then turned over to him. 'You were right—it wasn't the drugs.'

CHAPTER ELEVEN

'IT'S MY MUM.'

Unfortunately Penny hadn't come into the bathroom to join him in the shower later the next morning. They were up to deuce after a much more tender lovemaking session and Penny was fixing some breakfast while Ethan showered when the intercom buzzed. 'I know this sounds like I'm eighteen...'

'You want me to hide?' Ethan grinned as she pulled on her nightdress and then her dressing gown.

'Not hide, just don't come out of the bedroom,' Penny said. 'She'll tell Jasmine and, honestly, by the time we get back to work they'll all have us engaged or something.'

'Mum!' Penny opened the door and stood as her mum gave her a cuddle.

'I'm so sorry, Penny, I wish I'd been here. I told you not to try till after my trip.'

And there were so many things she could have said to that, but Penny buttoned her lip and forced a smile.

'How was the cruise?'

'It was amazing!' It must have been because Louise *looked* amazing! She was suntanned and relaxed-looking and wearing new clothes and jewellery, and her hair was a fabulous caramel colour and very well cut. 'I had the best time, Penny. You'd love it!'

'I think I might,' Penny said, because till her mother had set off, she'd never even considered one, but she was seeing the benefits now.

'All you do is eat and be pampered—I've got so much to tell you!'

And Ethan lay on the bed, reading magazines, listening as Penny did her best to limit his exposure to her mother's love life, because Penny kept asking her to describe islands, but her mum just kept talking about a man she had met. 'I go all the way to Greece and Bradley's from Melbourne and he's so romantic. One night—'

'Hold on a minute, Mum,' Penny interrupted. 'I'm just going to get changed.'

She brought Ethan in a coffee, which she would pretend she'd left in her room, not that her mother would notice. She was way too busy discussing Bradley and comparing the differences with Penny's father.

'I'm so sorry.'

'It's interesting.'

It was, and it became more so because Penny could not stop her mother from talking, and Ethan heard how useless her father had been and that maybe Louise had been a bit harsh in her summing up of *all* men to her daughters, because Bradley was nothing like that at all.

They were serious, in fact, he heard her tell Penny.

'It's a month, Mum.'

'And I'm old enough to know what I like and that this is right.'

'Well, why not just see how it goes now you're back?' He could hear Penny's wariness and then her mother's exasperation.

'Can't you just be happy for me, Penny?'

'Of course I am.'

But they all knew it was qualified and then the strain was back in Penny's voice, especially when her mother asked how she felt about losing the baby.

'It wasn't a baby, Mum! I got my period.' Ethan closed his eyes. Kate had been right—it was different for everyone, because Kate had had photos and named every embryo. 'It just didn't work.'

'Okay, Penny.'

They chatted some more and then with Penny promising to go round tomorrow she finally got her mother out of the door. Ethan looked up at Penny's strained features as she came through the bedroom door.

'Sorry about that.'

'No need to say sorry.'

'She just goes too far.' Penny let out an angry breath. 'I can't think of it as a baby.' Ethan was terribly aware suddenly that he was lying not in a bed but a minefield. 'I'd go mad otherwise, if I thought like that.'

'I know.'

'I bet she didn't ask Jasmine to hold off trying to conceive till she got back.' Ethan swallowed, thought it best not to say a thing, though was tempted to fire a quick SOS to his sister just in case he said the wrong thing. 'Well, she can go over there now and hear Jasmine's latest happy news.' Penny joined him on the bed. 'She's met the love of her life, apparently.'

'Bradley,' Ethan said, and she gave a little laugh.

She turned to him. 'I'm supposed to be happy for her.'

'Aren't you?'

Penny looked back at him. 'From past experience I really don't trust my mother's taste in men so no, I'm not going to clap hands and get

all excited. He's the first person she's seriously
dated since my father left.'

'Do you ever see him?'

'Never,' Penny said. 'And I've never wanted
to. I see enough of his sort at work and I've
stitched up enough of his sort's handiwork too.'
She didn't want to talk about her father. 'What
did you do while we were talking?' Penny asked.

'Read,' Ethan said. 'Had a little walk around
the bed, worked out that you rotate your wardrobe...'

'Of course I do,' Penny said. 'I haven't got time
to think what to wear each day.' She climbed off
the bed. 'I'm going to have a shower.'

'Good,' Ethan said. 'And I'll find you something to wear.'

'I can choose my own clothes, thank you.'

'You don't know where we're going.'

'Ethan, I don't want to go out.'

'Which is exactly why you should.'

Penny chose her own clothes, thank you very
much. A pair of shorts and a T-shirt and wedge

sandals and Ethan watched in amusement as she applied factor thirty to every exposed piece of skin. When they walked out of her smart townhouse and didn't head straight for his car, Penny actually felt a bit shaky.

'I've been inside too long.'

'I know you have.'

Really, since her walk on the beach with Jasmine it had been work and appointments and stopping at the supermarket on the way home, she told Ethan as they walked down to the beach.

'I'm a terrible wife even to myself,' Penny said, taking off her sandals and holding them as they walked down the path to the beach. 'I try to remember to make lots of meals and then freeze them and I always mean to make healthy lunches and take them in.'

'Same,' Ethan said.

'And I do it for one day, sometimes two.'

'That's why there's a canteen, Penny.' Ethan smiled. 'For all the people who have rotting vegetables in the drawer at the bottom of their fridge and didn't have time to make a sandwich, and if they did they don't have any super-healthy grain bread.'

Penny smiled. It was actually really nice to be out. It was a very clear day, the bay as blue and still as the sky, and the beach pretty empty. It was just nice to feel the sand beneath her feet and she thought of the last time she had been here with Jasmine and Simon, having hot flashes and carrying petrified hope and talking about wild flings with Ethan.

Penny glanced over at him, glad and surprised that the one thing she hadn't wanted that day had transpired.

'How come you ended up at Peninsula?' Penny asked.

'I wanted a change.' Ethan's voice was wry. 'I thought a nice bayside hospital would mean a nice laid-back lifestyle—I mean, given we don't have PICU and things.' He gave a shrug. 'I didn't count on catchments and that we'd get everything for miles around and then end up transferring them out.'

'You don't like it?'

'I love it,' Ethan mused. 'It just wasn't what I was expecting it to be—and I know that I don't do this sort of thing enough.' Ethan thought about it all for a long moment as they walked—thought about the wall of silence he had been met with because he hadn't been able to suddenly come back when Penny was sick. Thought about all that was silently expected of them. Ethan wasn't a rebel, just knew that there had to be more than work, and he told her that.

'You go out,' Penny said, because she'd heard that Ethan liked to party hard.

'I do,' Ethan said, 'but...' Just not lately. Ethan had once thought of days off counted in parties and bars and women and how much he could cram in. But since Phil's death it had all halted. Right now, just pausing on the beach on his one day off, Ethan actually felt like he'd escaped.

'I'm going to join a gym.' Penny broke into his thoughts.

'So you can feel guilty about not going?'

He made her smile because, yes, over the years she'd joined the hospital gym and the one near home many times.

'Why don't you just walk here more often?' Ethan suggested.

'Why don't you?'

They took the path off the beach that led into town and ordered brunch—smoked salmon and poached eggs on a very unhealthy white bread, washed down with coffee and fruit juice, and it was nice to sit outside and watch the world passing. Ethan was right, it was so good to be out, but being out meant exposure and after half an hour sitting at a pavement café she heard a woman call his name.

'Ethan.'

Penny looked up and it was the woman who had dropped him off that time, except she was pushing a stroller with a three-year-old and a very young baby.

'Kate.' Ethan smiled and looked down at his niece and nephew and gave them a wave then remembered to make the introductions. 'This is Penny from work and, Penny, this is my sister, Kate.'

'Of course you should join us,' Penny said when Kate insisted she didn't want to interrupt. She sat but when there wasn't a waiter to be found Ethan headed inside to order coffee and a milkshake for the three-year-old.

It was horribly awkward for Penny, because she and Kate were just so different; both lived close by yet both moved in completely different circles.

Both had a bit of what the other wanted.

'Days off?' Kate asked.

'Yes,' Penny answered. 'Well, I've been off sick, but I'm back tomorrow.'

'I'm sorry to hear that,' Kate said, aching at

the defensiveness in Penny's voice, because she knew so much more.

'Ethan said you had three children?'

'Yes, the eldest is at school,' Kate said, nodding towards the school over the street. 'You work in Emergency with Ethan?' she checked, as if she didn't already know. 'I think I saw you when I dropped Ethan off one morning.'

'That's right.' Penny did her best not to blush, because it had been the morning she had actually realised just how gorgeous Ethan was.

Yes, it was awkward because Penny just said as she always did, as little as possible about herself. If she'd only open up, Ethan thought when he returned, then Kate would tell her all about the hell she had gone through to get her three, but instead they talked about work and weather and things that didn't matter, till Kate had to go. 'I'll catch up with you soon, Ethan.' She gave her brother a friendly kiss on the cheek. 'It was lovely to meet you, Penny.'

'And you.'

'She seems nice,' Penny said.

'She is,' Ethan said, but if she'd just spoken properly to her, then Penny would know that Kate didn't just *seem* nice, she actually *was*.

Penny, Penny, Ethan sighed in his head. What to do?

'Shall we go to the movies?'

'The movies?' Penny frowned. 'I haven't been to the movies since…' She thought for a moment. 'I can't remember when.'

At her insistence, Penny bought the tickets and he went and got the popcorn and drinks and things, but as she walked over she saw him talking to a woman and a young boy and stopped walking.

The woman was being polite, but her face was a frozen mask. The young boy beside her was smiling up at Ethan and she just knew then that it was Justin. He looked like Ethan.

She was shaking a bit inside, her mind racing. She'd got it wrong with his sister; she couldn't keep jumping to the conclusion that every woman he spoke to he'd slept with. Penny made a great deal about putting the tickets into her purse, pretending to jump in surprise as Ethan came over.

'Okay?' Penny checked.

'Sure.'

She could tell he wasn't.

Still, the movie was a good one and it was so nice to sit in the darkness—so nice not to have to think. They sat at the back in a practically empty cinema and ate popcorn and just checked out of the world for a little while, which for Penny was bliss. It was nice too for Ethan to not go over and over the terse conversation with Gina. To just accept that Gina didn't want her ex-husband's cousin involved in her son's life.

He turned in the darkness to Penny about the same time she turned to him. There was the rustle of popcorn falling to the floor as they acted more like teenagers than a responsible couple in their thirties. After the movie Ethan wished he had brought the car as they walked quickly along the beach, almost running, not just to be together but away from problems each needed to face.

It felt so good to fall through the door, to lift her arms as he slid her out of her top, to undo the zipper of her shorts, as she did the same to him.

'Why did we leave it so long?' He was kissing her, not thinking of anything else but her mouth and her body and all the times they had missed, and how much better the boat would have been if he'd had Penny there with him.

'You know why.'

Ethan's head was in two places as he remembered what had kept them apart, but that problem had gone now and he just wasn't thinking, or rather he was thinking out loud, but before he had time to stop himself suddenly the words were out.

'Maybe it's for the best.'

CHAPTER TWELVE

'You didn't say that?' Kate grimaced. 'God, Ethan.'

'I can't believe I said it.' The once laid-back Ethan had his head in his hands as Kate grilled him further.

'What did she do?'

His look said it all because Penny had said the F word again, quite a few times, as she'd kicked him out.

'I'm not saying you have to tiptoe around her, but honestly, Ethan, it is the most awful time. Carl and I never row, but we have every time I've been on IVF, and if he'd said that...' Kate let out a long, angry sigh that told Ethan her reaction would have perhaps been as volatile as Penny's.

'I can understand you'd be upset if Carl said

it, but I didn't mean it like that,' Ethan said. 'I meant…' He stopped talking then.

'What?' his sister pushed.

'That I can barely get my head around a long-term relationship and having kids of my own, let alone going out with someone who was pregnant with someone else's child. When I said it was for the best I just meant that at least now we had a chance.'

'You need to tell her that.'

'You've met her,' Ethan told his twin. 'She's the most difficult, complicated…' And there it was, she was everything he wanted, the one woman who could possibly hold his attention. And she was still holding it fully on her first day back at work.

Penny was wearing a grey skirt with her cream sleeveless blouse but she'd lost weight around her hips and maybe he *was* a bit of a caveman because he wanted to insist she take some proper time off and haul her to his bed, and feed her and have sex with her and then watch late-night shows in his dark bedroom while she slept, while she healed. He wanted to take care of her. Instead, he had to stand and watch as she nitpicked her way through the department, upsetting everyone. Any minute soon he was going to have to step in.

'Why hasn't his blood pressure been done?' Her voice carried over the resuscitation room. Penny was checking the obs chart on her patient. She had ordered observations to be taken every fifteen minutes and when she saw that they hadn't been done for half an hour she called out to Vanessa.

'It has been done,' Vanessa said, taking the chart. 'Sorry, Penny, I just didn't write it down. It was one-eighty over ninety.'

'Which means nothing if it isn't written down.' Penny held her breath and told herself to calm down, but she'd told Vanessa about this a few times. 'You *have* to document.'

'I know.'

'Then why don't you do it?' Penny said, and

as she walked off, she was aware that Ethan was behind her. He tapped her smartly on the shoulder but she ignored him.

'Stop taking it out on the nurses.'

'I'm not,' Penny said. 'What's the point of Vanessa knowing the patient is hypertensive and not telling me or even writing it down? If he strokes out—'

'Penny.' He knew all that, knew that she was right, but he could see the dark shadows under her eyes and could feel her tense and too thin under his hand on her shoulder. 'I'm sorry for what I said.'

'I don't want to discuss that.'

'Tough.' She had marched to her office and Ethan had followed and stood with his back to the door. 'I said the wrong thing. I say the wrong thing a lot apparently.'

'You said how you felt.'

'How could I have when I don't even know how I feel?' Ethan couldn't contain it any longer and to hell with lousy timing, it had been lousy timing for him as well. 'I'm sorry that I didn't arrive in your life with a fully packed nappy bag, ready to be a father to another man's child.' Penny closed her eyes. 'Instead, I walked in on the end of a huge life decision you'd made.'

'I didn't make it lightly.'

'But I was supposed to,' Ethan said. 'I was supposed to be fine with it, delighted that you were pregnant, and for you I was, just not for us!'

And she was just so bruised and raw and angry and lost she didn't know how to respond anymore.

'Just leave it.'

'How can I leave it?' Ethan demanded. 'Because I'm trying to sort the two of us out and you're talking about going for it again.'

'No, I'm not.'

Today, Ethan wanted to add, but just stood there, trying to hold on to his temper, because only a low-life would have a row with a woman going through this. 'Okay, let's just leave it,'

Ethan said, 'but I will not have you taking it out on the nurses. You've upset Vanessa.'

'Vanessa knows me.' Guilt prickled down her spine. 'I've worked with Vanessa for years.'

'Hey,' Ethan snapped. 'Do you remember that guy I stitched who'd just had a remote control bounce off his skull?'

She had no idea what he was talking about. 'Well, maybe you weren't working that day, but he said the same. "She's never moaned, we've been married for years."' His eyes flashed at Penny. 'People will put up with so much, Penny, but not for ever.'

'I get that!' Penny screwed her eyes closed on tears. 'I've always been strict with observations, I've always been tough.'

'There's another word to describe you that's doing the rounds right now, Penny.'

'I know that. It's just been so intense.'

'I know that,' Ethan said, 'but the staff don't. I'm not going to stand back and let you take it out on them, Penny. Please.' He was trying to pull her up, trying to talk her down; he just wanted to take her home, but she didn't want him to and as he tried to take her in his arms Penny was backing off.

'I know it's been hell for you,' Ethan said.

'Well, it's over.' Penny swallowed down her pain. 'I just want to get back to my life, back to my career. I can't believe that I turned down a prom…' She stopped herself.

'Say it.'

Penny looked at him.

'It doesn't matter.'

'You know how I really hate that.' And so he waited.

'I turned down a promotion so that I could concentrate on IVF.'

'You mean you turned down my job?' Ethan checked, and she gave a tight shrug. Then he was on side with the masses—Penny could be such a bitch at times. 'Thanks a lot, Penny.'

She wanted to call him back, except he walked

out, and if that wasn't enough to be dealing with, a moment later there was a knock at her door.

'Hi, Lisa.' Penny gave a tight smile. 'It's not really a good time.'

'No, it isn't a good time,' Lisa said. 'My nurses work hard, Penny, and they put up with a lot and they do many extra things to help you that you probably don't even notice.' Penny swallowed as Lisa continued. 'But you might start to notice just how much extra they did for you when they stop.'

'It will be okay,' Jasmine said.

Penny had left work early, to Mr Dean's obvious displeasure, and the second she had got home she had rung her sister and said sorry, and Jasmine had come round. They'd had a cuddle when Jasmine had arrived at her door and, this time, when Penny had felt the swell in her sister's stomach, while it had hurt, overriding that Penny was happy for her sister and just so pleased to see her that she told Jasmine about work.

'I've upset all the nurses.'

'Penny!' Jasmine flailed between divided loyalties. 'You haven't been that bad. Lisa can be a cow at times—and Vanessa's always forgetting to write things down, but if you were more friendly, if people knew more what was going on in your life…'

'I don't know how to tell people.'

And Jasmine got that, because since she had been a little girl it had been Penny who had taken care of things, who had let her little sister open up to her about all the scary stuff going on with their parents and had said nothing about her own fears.

'You told Ethan.'

'Because I had to.'

'So how did the Neanderthal do?' Jasmine asked.

'He was great,' Penny said, and she let out a sigh as she remembered that day, how he'd stepped in when she'd broken down, how he'd actually said all the right things. 'Not just with the injections.'

'You like him?'

Penny nodded. 'And I just hurt him,' she said. 'I let it slip about the promotion.'

'You didn't just let it slip,' Jasmine said. 'You did what you always do whenever anyone gets close.'

'Probably,' Penny admitted.

'Try talking to him,' Jasmine said.

'I don't want to talk to him about this, though,' Penny said. 'It's all we talk about and I'm tired of it. I wish I'd met him without this damn IVF hanging over me. I want us to have a chance at normal.'

'Tell him, then,' Jasmine urged.

'I can't yet,' Penny admitted. 'I need to sort out myself first, work out how I feel about other things.' Penny took a deep breath. 'I've just been going round in circles and I can't anymore and

I'm not going to dump on Ethan. I need to think of myself.'

When Jasmine had gone she rang Mr Dean.

Told him she was struggling with some personal issues and that she was taking some time off.

Just let him put a word wrong now, Penny thought.

'That's fine, Penny.' Mr Dean must have heard the unvoiced warning in her tone, because he told her to take the two weeks of annual leave she had left and more if she needed it, and even though he could be very insensitive, for once he was incredibly careful not to say the wrong thing.

Unlike a certain someone, Penny thought as she stripped off her work clothes and headed for the shower.

Unlike Ethan.

Penny's eyes filled with tears then because part of what she liked about Ethan was that he did say the wrong thing and wasn't always careful at times, wasn't tentative and constantly wearing kid gloves around her, which she hated.

He'd never deliberately hurt her, he'd just been trying to say how he felt about her losing… Penny screwed her eyes closed, tried to block the pain, but she couldn't do it anymore. There wasn't a needle in sight but she let it all out then, folded up on the shower floor, crying and sobbing as she mourned. Because it wasn't just a failed IVF, she hadn't just got her period that horrible time. For a little while there she had thought she'd got her baby.

While she might feel better after a really good cry, Penny thought, she certainly didn't look better.

Huddled on the sofa in her nightdress, watching but not watching the news, Penny surveyed the damage. Yes, IVF was expensive, and she wasn't just talking dollars.

Penny rang her mum and had a nice talk with her, a really nice talk, because her mum told Bradley she was taking the call upstairs and they spoke for a good hour. Louise offered to come over but Penny didn't want her to.

Next.

Unable to say it, she fired off Ethan a text saying she was sorry for being such a bitch about his job.

And then he sent her a text with a photo attached—a big bear with a tiny dart in it.

Just a bruised ego—all mended now.

Which made her smile, and when a little while later her doorbell rang she wasn't sure if it was Ethan or her mum, but as she opened it, Penny knew her response would be the same.

'I really want to be on my own.'

'Why?' Ethan said. He'd come straight from work and was in his scrubs and looking far too gorgeous for someone feeling as drained as Penny did.

'Because I'm such good company.' She didn't need to tell him she was being sarcastic. He looked at her swollen eyes and lips and the little dark red dots on her eyelids and he couldn't let her close the door.

'I need to talk to you, Penny,' Ethan said. 'I lied to you.'

'That's fine.'

'You don't even want to know when I lied?'

'No,' Penny said. 'I want to think about me.' But she did let him in. Ethan pulled her into his arms for a cuddle but he felt her resistance and just wanted to erase it, wanted to take some of her hurt, but she simply wouldn't let him. 'I wish you'd spoken to my sister. Kate's been through it many, many times. I wish you'd let people in.'

'I wish I would too,' Penny said.

'Then why don't you?' He could see the confusion swirling in her eyes, guessed she was trying to answer that by herself. He was going to make her talk, was determined to sort things out, and he led her to the couch and sat down beside her. 'You don't have to keep it all in. It's not good for you. You said you didn't get upset when your dad left and then a few days later—'

'Oh, don't start.'

'I have started,' Ethan said.

'Of course I was upset when he left,' Penny said.

'You just couldn't show it.'

'No!' Penny said. 'Because Jasmine was sobbing herself to sleep, Mum was doing the same on the couch, and someone had to do the dishes and make Jasmine her lunch and...' She swallowed the hot choking fear she had felt then. 'How would falling apart have helped?'

'It might have stopped you falling apart now,' Ethan suggested. 'It might have meant your mother would have stepped up. It might have meant someone stepping in.'

'I'm not falling apart,' Penny said, and she meant it. 'I did that a couple of hours ago.'

He looked at her swollen face. 'I could have been there for you.'

'Oh, no,' Penny said. 'I'm so glad that you weren't.' She gave him a smile, a real one, because there were things she simply didn't want another person to see, and she actually felt better for her mammoth cry and was ready now to face another truth.

'So when did you lie?'

'I *was* serious about Caitlin.' The smile slid from her face when she didn't get the answer she was expecting. 'Not quite walking-up-the-aisle serious, but serious. And then Phil got sick and the thought of being married, having kids, leaving them behind?' He was honest. 'It just freaked me out.'

'I do understand. It is scary to think of being responsible for another person,' she admitted.

'But you want it,' Ethan said. 'You're brave enough to do it your own.'

'Not on my own,' Penny said, 'because even if we fight I do have my sister and mum, and if something happened to me, they'd be there.' She looked at him. 'I thought you were about to tell me you had a son.'

He gave her a barking-mad look.

'I saw you at the cinema.'

'That was Justin.'

'He looks like you,' Penny said, smiling now at her own paranoia.

'Phil looked like me,' Ethan said, then changed the subject because she was getting too close to a place that hurt. 'You do too much on your own.'

'Better than not doing it at all.' She smiled and nudged him, except Ethan didn't smile, and to her horror she watched him swallow, watched him struggle to get a grip, saw him pinch his nose and it was her arm around him now.

'Ethan?'

'Sorry.' He let out a slightly incredulous laugh, shocked how much was there just beneath the surface, how much he had just refused to let out.

'Is it Phil?'

He shook his head and again he got how the patients liked her because she sort of went straight to the really painful bit rather than tip-toeing around it. 'Justin?'

'If you get famous and they name a perfume after you, it won't be called Subtle, Penny.'

'No, it will be called Pertinent,' Penny said. 'You *need* to be there for him, Ethan.' And he nodded, rested his head in his hands, and Penny felt the tension in his shoulders, heard him struggle to keep his voice even as he gave a ragged apology. 'This was supposed to be about you.'

'How selfish of you.' Penny smiled.

'I don't know what to do—I've been trying to stay out of it but I can't. And it's not just the family stuff and that Gina's keeping him from his grandparents. The thing is, I know how he feels. It's like I'm looking at a mini-me. I saw him at the hospital, heard my aunt saying the same things she did to me when my father died—to be brave, bc strong. It's not what he needs to hear right now.'

'You can be there for him.'

'I don't want to go rushing in and make promises I might not keep,' Ethan admitted. 'I've never been able to commit myself to anything except work. Penny, I don't want to let him down.'

'You won't.' She saw him blink at the certainty in her voice. 'I know you won't let him down, precisely because you haven't rushed in. Just take your time and you'll work something out.'

'I don't know what, though.' He looked to where she was sitting and pulled her onto his lap, and this time she didn't resist when he pulled her in for a cuddle. 'So much for cheering you up.'

'You have, though.' Penny smiled and he smiled too. 'Thank you for everything,' Penny said. 'Not just the injections but…' she looked at the man who was still there despite all that had gone on these past weeks '…thank you for being my friend through this.'

'A bit more than a friend.' And to confirm it gave her a kiss. A kiss that seemed at odds with the way she was feeling, because there was this well of happiness filling her at what should have been the saddest of times.

'Are you wearing no knickers again?' Ethan smiled again and he had possibly the nicest mouth a man could have, and she was looking

into his hazel eyes and it hadn't just been manufactured hormones that had been raging that
time. Penny could fully see it now. It had been
lust, all the flush of a new romance, the big one,
because right now for Penny it was looking like
something a lot bigger than lust.

Something she'd never really felt before—an
L word that would probably be as shocking to
Ethan as the F word had been to Jasmine, and
if that mouth returned to hers now, she might
be tempted later to say so, and again it was just
too much and too soon.

'You need to go,' Penny said.

'Do I?'

'Yes,' Penny said, 'because I want to go to bed
and have sex with you and I want to get up tomorrow and do it again, and then I want you to
take me out tomorrow night, but I think I need
to think about things properly. I need to work
some stuff out.'

'And you can't do that with me?'

Penny looked at him and, no, she didn't want

to try to do this with Ethan—her fertility issues were conversations that should be had far
later along in a relationship, dark places a couple
might visit later that had instead been thrust on
them at the beginning.

'It's a girl thing,' Penny said, because with or
without Ethan in her future she needed to properly know how she felt. And as to the other issue,
the L one—well, she didn't need him by her side
to work that out.

Penny already knew.

So much for a wild fling—of all the times to
go and fall in love with someone.

'I could make love to you on the sofa and then
leave,' Ethan said, cupping her naked bottom
and making her laugh.

'I suppose that might be a compromise.'

He kissed her again, pulled her around on his
lap so she was facing him, and his hands were
everywhere and so too were hers. 'I'm crazy
about you, Penny.'

'I know,' she said, kissing him back and trying to hold on to a word he might not be ready to hear. 'I'm crazy about you too.'

Her hand went to his back pocket, which gave him lovely access to her neck. She could feel his tongue, his mouth most definitely leaving evidence that hers hadn't been about to, but it was bliss and she had a whole two weeks off, so she let him carry on, working her neck and his hands stroked her breasts as she slid the condom on him.

'You'll call me if you need me,' Ethan said as she sank herself down onto him.

'You'll call me too,' Penny said, locked in an erotic embrace, hardly able to breathe. 'But not for this.'

'Penny.' He was lifting his hips and thrusting into her, protesting her impossible rules.

'I mean it,' Penny panted, because she could bury herself in Ethan and stay there forever, just as he was burying himself deep in her now.

Yes, a good cry and a good orgasm and Penny felt a whole lot better as she kissed him goodbye at her door. Still stuck on deuce but with play suspended.

Penny *was* going to sort herself out.

And so too would Ethan.

CHAPTER THIRTEEN

'PENNY!' KATE SMILED as she walked past the café and ignored Penny's burning cheeks.

'Oh, hi,' Penny said, as if she just happened to be sitting there at a quarter to nine in the morning, as if she hadn't been looking up school times on the internet, as if she hadn't spent forty minutes trying to cover the marks on her neck and her puffy eyes. 'How are you?'

'Good.' Kate smiled. 'Though I could do with one of them.' She nodded to Penny's coffee and, yes, she'd love to join her and, yes, Penny thought, it was another woman she needed for this and this link was thanks to Ethan.

'How's work?' Kate asked, taking a seat.

'I'm taking some time off.' She told her why and Penny realised that Kate probably already knew.

'Did Ethan tell you?'

'Do I have to answer that?'

'No.' Penny shook her head.

'Then I won't.'

Kate had been there and knew, though she couldn't have a second coffee, not at the café anyway because the baby needed feeding. In truth, she shouldn't really have stopped for the first, but she'd been where Penny was.

'We could take a coffee back to mine,' Kate suggested, 'and talk there.'

It *was* another woman Penny needed, one who'd been there and knew—who knew it so well that she took phone calls for a support group.

'Everyone was pregnant when I started trying,' Kate said, making up bottles for Dillon a little while later as Penny sat at the kitchen table.

It *was* so nice to talk and to hold someone else's baby and not feel guilty for shedding tears. She'd always tried to smile with Jasmine and friends, and say, no, no, she was fine. It was nice to hold one and have a little weep.

'I think I've gone a bit mad,' Penny admitted.

'It's par for the course.'

Penny looked at Dillon and though she'd never be disappointed with a boy, Penny admitted to herself that deep down she would have loved a girl too. Oh, a boy would be fantastic, but she'd have loved a mini-Penny. A little girl who she could do everything right by and fix the world for, who she could unashamedly show all the love that bubbled and fizzed inside.

But she could do it for herself too, Penny realised.

'I've just had a text,' Kate said a little while later. 'My brother's coming around.'

'I'll go, then.'

She thanked Kate for the morning and they had a hug and she handed back little Dillon. It wasn't that she didn't want to see Ethan, it was more there was something she was ready to face and she wanted to face it alone. Penny headed to the beach and walked for a while, adding up all the months, all the years, all the time she'd lost trying. She was ready to stop and so she said it out loud—but to herself first.

'I'm not going to be a mum.' She actually didn't cry as she said it, just felt relief almost as she let go of something she had never had, anger shifting towards acceptance; sadness a constant ache but one she could now more readily wear.

Yes, times alone were needed for both of them, yet Kate was the strange conduit that linked them.

'She's been here.' He could just tell, when about ten minutes after Penny left he was at his sister's door and Kate was blushing and flustered when she answered.

'Why do you say that?'

'Because I can smell her perfume,' Ethan said.

'You really have got it bad,' Kate said. 'What did you do to her neck?'

Ethan wasn't going to answer that one, so he

asked a question instead. 'What was she talking about?'

'Not about you,' Kate said, then added, 'She's really nice.'

Not *seems*, Ethan noted—finally, it would appear, Penny was letting people in.

'She is.'

'Well, I hate to chuck you out so soon, but I've got nothing done today and I'm on fruit duty at playgroup.' Kate was putting sandals onto her daughter's feet. The baby was asleep and instead of letting her wake him, as usually Ethan would, he offered to watch him instead.

'Are you sure?' Kate checked. 'There's a bottle in the fridge if he wakes up.'

'Go.'

And later he sat with Dillon on his lap and stared at a very little man who would, God willing, grow up.

And, Ethan realised, taking out his phone, it was time for him to as well.

Just not yet.

He made every decision alone—it was simply the way he was, but instead of ringing who he meant to, he dialled Penny.

She probably wouldn't pick up.

'Hi.'

'Hi, Penny,' he said. 'What are you doing?'

'Sitting on the beach. What about you?'

'Watching my nephew. Kate's at playgroup.' He took a deep breath. 'I'm going to ring Gina.'

'That's good.'

'I think I need to say sorry first, for how the family has been.' He was really just thinking out loud.

'Maybe,' Penny said, 'but are you ringing on behalf of the family?'

'No.'

'You could just keep it more about you,' Penny said, and they chatted for a while about what he might say till the baby on his lap decided that a bottle might be a good idea, and Penny could hear his little whimpers in the background.

'You'd better go,' Penny said. 'It sounds like the baby needs feeding.'

As he hung up the phone he sat for a moment, wondering if he'd upset her with the baby crying and everything, but she'd seemed fine. It had been their first full conversation without a mention of babies.

'Apart from you,' he said to Dillon as he headed to the fridge.

Ethan offered the baby his bottle but he spat out the cold milk so Ethan warmed it up. 'It was worth a try.' He grinned at his new friend and they settled back down on the sofa. There was no putting it off any longer and Ethan again picked up his phone.

'Gina...' He took a deep breath. 'It's Ethan.' He was met with a very long silence. 'I'm really sorry for all that the family has put you through.'

'You didn't.'

'No,' he said. 'But I do know what happened and I know too what Jack and Vera can be like.' He took a long breath. 'But I'm not ringing about them, I'm ringing about Justin. I lost my dad around the same age.'

'I know.'

They chatted for a bit and it was awkward at first and there was a long stretch of silence when he made his suggestion. 'I was thinking, if it's okay with you, I could get Justin his football membership. I can't take him every week, it depends on the roster, but...' He thought of Penny, because he so often did and, yes, she'd swap now and then and so too would the others.

This he could do.

Would do.

'I would be able to take Justin to most games.'

'He'd love that,' Gina said. 'But...' She hesitated for a moment.

'I'm not starting something I won't see through,' Ethan said. 'I'm not saying I'm never going to move, but I will be there for him. I wouldn't be offering otherwise.'

Only that wasn't what Gina was hesitating about. 'Maybe you could take him to his grandparents' after the match, but not every week. Maybe he could stay over?' Gina let out a sigh. 'But I can't face picking him up.'

'I can do that,' Ethan said. 'We can work out times.'

'Would you talk to Vera and Jack first?' Gina said. 'I don't want Justin going there and being told what a terrible person I am.'

'I'll talk to them,' Ethan said. 'And if it's not working out, I'll talk to them again, but whatever happens there, I'll be around for Justin.'

They chatted some more and it was agreed he would ring Justin and tell him the good news that night. When Ethan hung up the phone he looked into the solemn eyes of his nephew.

'How did I do?'

He got no answer.

'When you're a bit bigger I might take you to the football too.' He got a smile for that and again his mind tripped back to Penny. 'I'll be the mad uncle.'

And so the weekend came around and he

picked up a six-year-old with a pinched, angry face. He knew that look only too well and sat where they always had, only this time without Phil.

And they shouted at the opposition and the umpire and let off a bit of a steam, but instead of talking about the game on the way to Justin's grandparents' they spoke about what mattered.

'Well, if he wanted to live so much then he should have tried harder,' Justin said, because he was tired of hearing that his dad had tried so hard to be there for him. And he got to be six and very angry instead of being told to be brave and strong. And maybe Penny has sprayed Ethan with some Pertinence before he left because instead of being subtle, instead of dropping him off at his Vera and Jack's and hoping for the best, Ethan warned him how things might be.

'They're upset,' Ethan said, 'and you remind them of your dad, and it's just so hard on everyone.' He blew out a breath because there was just so much hurt all around, but so much love too.

'They hate my mum.'

'They don't,' Ethan said, and then corrected himself, because it was Justin who was dealing with this. 'Well, if they do, you shouldn't have to hear it. You tell me if they say anything that hurts. And if they are less than nice about her, it's because they don't know your mum,' Ethan said. 'She's great.'

He saw the smile lift the edge of Justin's lips as finally someone in the Lewis family said something nice about his mum.

Yes, Ethan decided, having dropped Justin off—this he could do.

CHAPTER FOURTEEN

'MORNING, ETHAN.' VANESSA was just coming on duty and smiled when she saw him, but then pulled a face. 'I'm guessing, from the state of you, that you're going off duty?'

Finishing up a week of nights, Ethan was aware that he probably wasn't looking his best. He had meant to shave before he'd come on last night, and had also meant to shave the night before that too. 'So, if you're going off duty…' Vanessa said, looking at the board that Lisa was filling in—it showed all the on-take doctors and who was on duty today. 'Oh, no!' Vanessa said as she watched Lisa write 'Penny Masters' in red. 'She's back.'

'She will be soon,' Lisa teased the nurses. 'Party's over for you lot.'

'Tell me about it. Who knows what her problem is,' Vanessa groaned, and Ethan wanted to tell them to give her a break, that the two of them had no idea what Penny was going through.

But Penny would hate that.

She was just this tough little thing choosing to go it alone, and for the last couple of weeks he'd had to force himself to respect that while trying to sort out how he felt about IVF and babies and things. Ethan still didn't know. He couldn't work out how he felt about dating someone who wanted a baby, oh, say, about nine months from now.

He'd bought flowers for the first time in his unromantic life and they were waiting in her office, along with an invitation for dinner. Maybe they could just take it slowly, start at the beginning without those blasted needles hanging over them.

Though he'd rather liked giving them!

Play was resuming, Ethan thought with a smile.

He heard the bell from Triage and Lisa stopped writing on the board and sped off with Ethan following. They got outside to find nurses trying to get an unconscious woman from the back seat of a car onto a trolley as her panicked husband shouted for them to hurry up. Security was nowhere to be seen.

'What happened?' Ethan asked the man.

'I just came home from work and I couldn't wake her...' The man was barefoot and jumping up and down on the spot. As his wife was placed on the trolley Ethan tried to get some more information, but apart from a urine infection there was nothing wrong with her, the agitated husband said.

'You're going to have to move your car,' Lisa told him as they started to move the patient inside, but he ignored her, instead running alongside his wife.

'You need to move your car,' Ethan said, because even if it sounded a minor detail, it wasn't if there was an ambulance on its way in with another sick patient.

'Just sort my wife out!' the man roared at Ethan. 'Stop worrying about the car.' There was a minor scuffle; the man fronted up to Ethan, fear and adrenaline and panic igniting. Ethan blocked the man's fist, but Ethan was angry too.

'Man up!' Ethan said. 'You want me to stand here fighting, or do you want me to sort out your wife? Go and move your car.'

He did so, but as they sped the woman through, the usually laid-back Ethan, who let things like that go, glared over at Lisa.

'Where the hell was Security?'

Lisa didn't answer.

'I want that reported.'

'He's just scared.'

'Yeah, well, we're all scared at times.'

They were now at the doors to Resus and Ethan was dealing with the patient, who was responding to pain and her pupils were reacting. He could smell what was wrong—there was the familiar smell of ketones on her breath. Lisa was attaching her to monitors as Ethan quickly found a vein and took bloods. 'Add a pregnancy test,' Ethan said, because she was of childbearing age and a diabetic crisis could be dangerous for any foetus. By the time the husband returned from parking his car there was saline up and Lisa was giving the patient her first dose of insulin. His anger was fading, but still it churned.

'Are you all right, Ethan?' Lisa checked.

'Sure.'

'I'll do an incident form after...'

'Forget it.' He gave a small smile that said he had overreacted.

'Touched a nerve, did it?' Lisa smiled back.

'Must have,' Ethan said.

He thought of his own fear as he'd raced to get to his cousin, yet it wouldn't have entered his head to front up to anyone, and he thought of Kate, who had done the right thing and not just left the car, even though she must so badly have wanted to. 'I want to know where Security was, though,' Ethan said, and then got back to the patient. The medics were on their way down but for now Ethan went in to speak with the husband.

'I'll come in with you,' Lisa said.

'No need,' Ethan said.

'I wasn't offering.' Lisa had worked there a very long time and gave him a smile that told him there was no way she was leaving the two of them in the same room.

'Come on, then.'

They walked in and the man was sitting in there, his head in his hands.

'Mr Edmunds.' Ethan looked at the patient sheet that had been handed to him.

'Mark.' He looked up. 'Sorry about before.'

Ethan would deal with that later. He was actually glad Lisa had insisted on coming in as there was still this strange surliness writhing inside Ethan and he looked down at the patient card again for a moment before talking.

'Your wife, Anna, did you know she was diabetic?'

Mark shook his head. 'No…she's been fine, well, tired, but like I said, she thought she had a urine infection.'

Ethan nodded. 'One of the signs is passing urine a lot but we're checking for any infection.' He explained things as simply as he could to the very confused and very scared man—that his wife had type one diabetes and she was in ketoacidosis—her glucose was far too high and would be slowly brought down. But it affected everything and she would be very closely watched, and while she was very sick, he expected her to soon be well.

'She'll still be diabetic?'

'Yes.' Ethan nodded. 'But she'll be taught to manage it and this will hopefully be the worst it ever is.' Ethan took a breath. 'Is there any chance that your wife might be pregnant?'

'We're trying.'

'Okay,' Ethan said.

'Would it damage the baby?'

'Let's just wait for results and then we'll see

what we're dealing with. Do you want to come in and see your wife?'

Mark nodded and then said it again. 'I am sorry about earlier.'

'And I accept your apology,' Ethan said. 'But there is no place for that sort of carry-on here.'

'I was just—'

'Not an excuse,' Ethan broke in. 'There were two women there and your fist wasn't looking where it was going. We've got doctors here who are barely five foot…'

Yes, there was his problem—everything went back to Penny.

But, hell, Ethan thought, it could have been Penny on duty and she could have been pregnant, and he stood up and walked out and took a deep breath.

'Where was Security?' Ethan asked Lisa.

'Over in the car park,' Lisa said. 'Someone was trying to break into a car. They can't be everywhere, Ethan.'

He knew that, but he wanted them everywhere,

wanted two burly guards and an Alsatian walking alongside Penny at all times.

Maybe he was a caveman after all.

CHAPTER FIFTEEN

YES, SHE HAD always rotated her clothes, mixing and matching her outfits with precision, changing them with the seasons. Not anymore. Today she had *chosen* a floral dress that buttoned at the front. Instead of low, flat heels, she wore sandals, and because she hadn't been meticulous with her factor thirty, Penny's legs were sun-kissed and she wore her hair loose.

She smiled as she walked into work and Ethan, tired after his night shift, chatting to the medics, noticed the glow in her and had a feeling her decision had been made and that there were embryos about to be taken out of storage in the very near future.

'Morning, Vanessa,' Penny said as she walked past.

'Er, morning, Penny.'

'Hi, Lisa.'

'Penny.'

Penny swallowed. 'Lisa, can I have a word with you, please?'

It was the hardest word and Lisa gave her a smile as they moved into an empty cubicle, and Penny said it. 'I've been going through some things and I should never have brought it to work. It was just...' And she did what Jasmine had advised all along and what Penny had thought she would never do—let Lisa know what had been going on.

'Well, you can't really leave your hormones at home.' Lisa smiled. 'You could have said.'

'I know.'

'I am discreet.'

'I know that too,' Penny said. 'I'll have a word with Vanessa and apologise. Anyone else?' And then Penny gave a guilty smile. 'Should I just call a staff meeting?'

Yes, it really was the hardest, hardest word

because sometimes when you had to say it, it meant that you'd really hurt someone.

'I'm so sorry, Vanessa.' Penny saw the red cheeks and the flash of tears in her colleague's eyes and it wasn't actually the blood pressure she hadn't written down or the delays in medication that were the problem. There was another morning Penny hadn't properly apologised for, and though she didn't want to play the sympathy card, Penny did want Vanessa to know that her outburst hadn't been aimed at her.

Penny took her into an interview room.

'You were right to come and get me that morning and let me know what was happening. I know you'd never leave a patient and that Raj was there. I wasn't angry at you—I was just upset. When you came to find me I'd just got my period,' Penny said. 'I'd been trying for a baby and I thought I was finally pregnant.' And, no, she didn't tell her that for twenty-four hours she had been pregnant, neither did she say anything about the IVF, but it was enough for Vanessa to put her arms around her. Penny gave a little self-conscious wriggle, but then found out that it was nice sometimes to have a friend and be held.

Ethan watched them walking out of the inter-view room, smiling and chatting, and he excused himself and walked over.

'Morning, Penny.'

'Morning.'

'Nice break?'

'Very.'

'What did you get up to?'

'Not much.' How lovely it was to say that.

'Glad to be back?'

'Not yet.' Penny took a deep breath. 'I'm sorry I've been such a cow to work with.' Even though he knew why, she still felt she ought to say it here in the workplace and not just to Ethan. 'I should have recorded my apology before I came back to work. You're the third and I haven't even got halfway down the corridor.'

'Maybe you could ask the receptionist to play it over the loudspeaker?' Ethan grinned.

She walked off to her office and turned and flashed that smile but he didn't follow at first.

He just stood there thinking, because he knew how he felt now, and he checked with himself for a moment and the answer was still the same so he headed to her office to tell her.

'I would have loved your baby.' Ethan stood at the door and whether it was the wrong or right thing to say, he told her what he now knew.

'Ethan…'

'I'm not just saying that.' He wasn't and he told her why. 'I know you're going to go for it again,' Ethan said, 'I could see it when you walked in. I'll tell you this, if you were pregnant now, if it had worked out for you, well, I might have taken a while to come around but I would have, because it wouldn't change the way I feel. It's just taken a bit of a time for me to understand that.'

'I'm not going for it again.' She saw him frown. 'This is Tranquil Penny.'

'Oh.' He came over and took her in his arms and introduced himself. 'Pleased to meet you.'

Then he frowned. 'What do you mean, you're not going to try again?'

'I can't have children.' She'd practised saying it, not just to Ethan but at other times in her future. 'I know I might want to try again someday, but now I just want a break from it—I want lots of sex for sex's sake, preferably with you.' She reached into her bag and took out a packet of pills and waved them. 'It's probably overkill— left to their own devices my ovaries squeeze out two, maybe three eggs a year—but I'm taking the pressure off.'

She gave him a smile. 'Yes, please, to dinner.' He kissed her and he had never been so pleased to kiss a woman, just relieved to find her mouth and what had been missing in every other mouth he had kissed.

Here it was, the love he hadn't been looking for.

'I'm going home to sleep,' Ethan said.

'Not yet,' Penny grumbled.

'I am, and then I'm going to set my alarm so

I've time to tidy up in case I end up bringing my date back.' He gave her a smile. 'You've never seen my home.'

Penny blushed. Yes, there was a lot to get to know and lots of fun to be had before a guy like Ethan might settle down. And it might never happen, but she wanted him in a way she never had. There was a love inside Penny so much bigger than this kiss. A love that crowded out so many other things, and she just had to hold on to her feelings a bit, not terrify him with them by jumping in too soon.

'Or maybe...' Ethan said, and he undid a couple of buttons and had a peek and she was in coral, his favourite '...we could skip the restaurant and eat at my place?'

'What's for dinner, Ethan?'

They had the tiniest of histories, but it was enough to make the other smile.

'That all depends on what you pick up at the supermarket on your way home from work,' Ethan said.

And he glimpsed then a future and there would be no remote-control flinging because they would look out for each other, argue and tease each other, and then kiss and make up and not let things fester.

'Do you want to go to the football on Sunday?'

'No!' Penny pulled a face; she could think of nothing worse, but then it clicked. 'Are you going with Justin?'

'It will be our second week,' Ethan said.

'Gina agreed?'

'More than that. Afterwards I'm taking him to my aunt and uncle's and he's staying the night, and then in the morning I'll go and collect him and take him back to his mum's. We'll be doing that a couple of times a month and it's working out well.'

'That's some commitment.' Penny smiled at her commitment-phobe.

'I'm getting good at them.'

Yes, there was still a lot she didn't know about Ethan, because as he stood there looking at her he was doing the maths. She was thirty-five and at a rate of two to three eggs a year there weren't a whole lot of chances, but he was prepared to take them now. Ethan picked up the pill pack she was still holding and, just as Penny had with the needles to get what she wanted, he faced his fears over and over, twenty-eight times, in fact.

He punched each pill into the sink, even the sugar-coated ones, and then turned on the tap and watched them swirl in the water. Then he broke out in a sweat because it was *him* now talking about making babies when he'd never thought he might.

'I've got more at home.'

'I want whatever happens,' Ethan said. 'And I don't want to take away even one of your chances.'

'And I don't want to ruin this,' Penny said. They were chasing the same dream from different directions, both terrified to miss or even to clash and blow them apart. Penny was standing at the silver lining of acceptance that there

might never be babies, and Ethan was just starting to accept that there might be. 'I don't want
you to find out you do want babies after all and
then be disappointed.'

And he was the most honest, sexiest, funni-
est man she had ever met, even as he voiced her
unspoken fears. 'And then go off with someone
years younger…'

'Ha, ha,' Penny said, because they could talk
about things, tell each other things and, yes, they
could tease each other too. 'Someone soft and
curvy and cute.'

'Did I really used to go for cute?' Ethan smiled.
And he looked at her and he knew where his
heart was. 'Actually,' Ethan said as he faced another of his fears, 'for one hot mess you'd make
a very cute bride.'

She blinked at him.

'I want to see Menopausal Penny and I want
you to see Midlife Crisis Ethan.'

'So do I.' She was kissing him again. 'Going

out in your sports car and joining a gym and things.'

'And if there are no babies, we'll be the mad aunt and uncle who spoil all their nieces and nephews but make their parents jealous as we go off on cruises and travel around the world. But,' Ethan said, 'if we're really clucky, we'll move to America and adopt little twin monkeys.'

'And dress them in tutus.'

'No,' Ethan said, because it was his future they were planning too. 'Not the boy one.'

EPILOGUE

'IT'S CALLED A spontaneous pregnancy,' her GP explained as Penny sat there, stunned. 'Some women do get pregnant naturally after IVF.'

It would seem so.

Penny honestly didn't know how she felt.

She'd imagined hearing she was pregnant so many times, but now that it was here, she actually didn't know how to deal with the news.

They had just returned from their honeymoon—Louise had given them the cruise bug and they had sailed around the Mediterranean, getting brown and being spoiled. Penny closed her eyes at the thought of the champagne and the things she had eaten, though now, when she thought about it, she hadn't really indulged that much.

'We nearly didn't go,' Penny admitted as she chatted to the doctor. She'd thought they'd have to call it off because Mr Dean had told them that they couldn't both take annual leave at the same time.

'We're hardly going to go on separate honeymoons,' Ethan had said—that was how they had announced their news—and given Ethan didn't actually have any annual leave and would be taking it unpaid, they could afford a locum to cover him.

'Be glad that you had your cruise.' Her GP smiled. 'Because you won't be doing that sort of thing for a while.'

And Penny was glad that they had, so glad, because they'd had nearly a year of just them and it had been amazing—dating for all of a week before Penny had put her house on the market and she and the cat had moved in with him, then just getting to know each other and learning how to laugh and to love.

Penny drove home. She was supposed to be

getting her hair done as it was her mother's wedding in a few hours' time, but instead she'd have to make do with heated rollers.

She just had to see Ethan, had to find out how he would take the news.

'Your hair's nice,' Ethan said when she got back. He was in the bathroom, shaving, the cat sitting by the sink watching him.

'I didn't get my hair done.' Penny had to laugh.

'Oh,' Ethan said. 'Well, it still looks nice. Where did you go?' He saw her hesitate and he pretty much guessed she'd been to her GP.

Penny had been fantastic and absolutely adored Jasmine's little baby girl, Amelia, and they'd just found out that Kate was going to try for a fourth. There were so many friends and relations getting pregnant that Ethan was noticing and he was starting to feel little pinpricks of disappointment when Penny's period rarely came.

And not just for Penny.

He liked the time spent with Justin, and Penny was good with him too. He wanted now what

Penny had wanted—a baby—though he couldn't really tell her that. No doubt soon they'd be off to America to look at little monkeys, but first...

'You'll be all right at the wedding?' He rinsed his face and then turned round. 'You're all right with your mum and Bradley?'

'Apart from his name,' Penny said. 'And do they have to be so affectionate in public?'

She was the oddest person he had ever met and he loved her all the more for it. And maybe the timing wasn't right, maybe he should bring it up after the wedding because he didn't want to upset her beforehand, but right or wrong he said what was on his mind.

'If you want to go again...'

'Go again?'

'On IVF,' Ethan said. 'I'd be fine with that.'

'You're sure?' Penny's eyes narrowed. 'That doesn't sound very enthusiastic.'

'Okay.' He tried again. 'Why don't *we* go on IVF?' He thought for a moment. 'That makes me sound like Gordon.' And then he was serious. 'If you want to then so do I.'

'What do you want, Ethan?'

'I can't believe I'm saying this,' Ethan admitted. 'But I'd like to try for a baby…' He rushed into his 'but if it doesn't work then I won't be disappointed' speech, but she halted him. There was no need for that. She loved it that he wanted this too, that it wasn't something she was foisting on them too soon.

'We don't need to try,' Penny said. 'I've just come from the doctor's.'

He was scared to get too excited, just in case it was like last time, only it was nothing like last time.

'I'm thirteen weeks,' Penny said, and she watched his reaction as it sank in that while they'd been busy with weddings and football matches and honeymoons and juggling work and falling deeper and deeper in love, she'd been pregnant.

'Can we tell people?' Ethan asked.

'I guess,' Penny said, because they were out of the first trimester. 'But not just yet. It's Mum's day today.'

And it was just as well she didn't get her hair done because it would have been messed up anyway as they were soon off to bed to celebrate. Ethan had the good sense to set the alarm just in case they got a bit carried away.

'Can't be late for your mum's wedding,' he said as a very tanned Penny stripped off.

They were on two sets to one, with Ethan winning, and each game spent an awful lot of time at deuce.

Record times!

'Hey, I bet when you were fantasising about having your wild fling with me,' Ethan said as he dropped his towel, 'you never imagined it ending up like this.'

'No,' Penny said, because the best she had been able to imagine then had been a shocked reaction and a baby that wasn't his.

The truth was so much better.

* * * * *

Mills & Boon® Large Print
Medical

February

MIRACLE ON KAIMOTU ISLAND	Marion Lennox
ALWAYS THE HERO	Alison Roberts
THE MAVERICK DOCTOR AND MISS PRIM	Scarlet Wilson
ABOUT THAT NIGHT…	Scarlet Wilson
DARING TO DATE DR CELEBRITY	Emily Forbes
RESISTING THE NEW DOC IN TOWN	Lucy Clark

March

THE WIFE HE NEVER FORGOT	Anne Fraser
THE LONE WOLF'S CRAVING	Tina Beckett
SHELTERED BY HER TOP-NOTCH BOSS	Joanna Neil
RE-AWAKENING HIS SHY NURSE	Annie Claydon
A CHILD TO HEAL THEIR HEARTS	Dianne Drake
SAFE IN HIS HANDS	Amy Ruttan

April

GOLD COAST ANGELS: A DOCTOR'S REDEMPTION	Marion Lennox
GOLD COAST ANGELS: TWO TINY HEARTBEATS	Fiona McArthur
CHRISTMAS MAGIC IN HEATHERDALE	Abigail Gordon
THE MOTHERHOOD MIX-UP	Jennifer Taylor
THE SECRET BETWEEN THEM	Lucy Clark
CRAVING HER ROUGH DIAMOND DOC	Amalie Berlin

May

GOLD COAST ANGELS: BUNDLE OF TROUBLE	Fiona Lowe
GOLD COAST ANGELS: HOW TO RESIST TEMPTATION	Amy Andrews
HER FIREFIGHTER UNDER THE MISTLETOE	Scarlet Wilson
SNOWBOUND WITH DR DELECTABLE	Susan Carlisle
HER REAL FAMILY CHRISTMAS	Kate Hardy
CHRISTMAS EVE DELIVERY	Connie Cox

June

FROM VENICE WITH LOVE	Alison Roberts
CHRISTMAS WITH HER EX	Fiona McArthur
AFTER THE CHRISTMAS PARTY…	Janice Lynn
HER MISTLETOE WISH	Lucy Clark
DATE WITH A SURGEON PRINCE	Meredith Webber
ONCE UPON A CHRISTMAS NIGHT…	Annie Claydon

July

HER HARD TO RESIST HUSBAND	Tina Beckett
THE REBEL DOC WHO STOLE HER HEART	Susan Carlisle
FROM DUTY TO DADDY	Sue MacKay
CHANGED BY HIS SON'S SMILE	Robin Gianna
MR RIGHT ALL ALONG	Jennifer Taylor
HER MIRACLE TWINS	Margaret Barker